Take Me
With You

Take Me
With You

CAROLYN MARSDEN

CANDLEWICK PRESS

Copyright © 2010 by Carolyn Marsden

First edition 2010

Library of Congress Cataloging-in-Publication Data

Marsden, Carolyn.
Take me with you / Carolyn Marsden. — 1st ed.
p.   cm.
Summary: Raised in an Italian orphanage in the years following
World War II, a biracial girl named Susanna and her best friend, Pina,
want to be adopted but fear being separated.
ISBN 978-0-7636-3739-2
[1. Adoption — Fiction. 2. Friendship — Fiction.
3. Abandoned children — Fiction. 4. Orphans — Fiction.
5. Racially mixed people — Fiction.
6. Italy — History — 1945–1976 — Fiction.]   I. Title.
PZ7.M35135Tak 2010
[Fic] — dc22   2009038053

09 10 11 12 13 14 MVP 10 9 8 7 6 5 4 3 2 1

Printed in York, PA, U.S.A.

This book was typeset in ITC Esprit.

Candlewick Press
99 Dover Street
Somerville, Massachusetts 02144

visit us at www.candlewick.com

For my own two girls

Strangers

STRANGERS HAD COME TO THE *CHIESA.*

Susanna stood taller on the wooden steps. There, she and about thirty other girls pressed close to warm themselves in the chilly, incense-sweet air. They waited patiently to sing their parts in the Latin Mass.

Today, besides the usual old ladies in black dresses, there were two young couples.

"So *short,*" whispered Elvira, nodding at the couple on the left.

"But maybe rich. Very rich," said Antonetta. "Look—the woman has fur trim on her coat."

"Looks like fox fur," Elvira said. "It's red."

"You should know about foxes," Susanna whispered.

Elvira had red hair, the same rusty, burnished color as the fur trim.

Suor Anna shook her head at them and frowned, her long, crooked finger to her lips. She was the head nun, and very old. She wore the black habit of the nuns, the huge, round white collar around her neck. Her finger was encircled by a gold wedding band, because she, like the other nuns, was a Bride of Christ.

Fox-Fur Lady's husband had a balding head and nice, light eyes.

Attention was now on the other couple on the far side of the *chiesa*. Everyone stood up on tiptoe. Susanna shifted the waist of her black skirt so the button squarely faced the back.

The woman wore a dress with big flowers, like a garden blooming across her large body. How had she gotten so fat? Susanna wondered. Since the war, Italy had not had enough food.

Her husband, in a plain brown suit like soil waiting to be planted, was very thin. Maybe she ate his food and her own too.

"They're here to adopt someone," pronounced Carla. "My parents told me that the nuns were arranging adoptions."

Adoptions? The word reverberated in the cold air. Susanna rocked against Pina, who stood next to her. Did that mean that some of them might go to a home of their very own?

More than ten years ago, all of the girls standing on the wooden steps had been brought to the *Istituto di Gesù Bambino* as babies. Some had been orphans. Some had had mothers or other family members who couldn't keep them. The nuns had cared for them all this time.

Now some girls might leave.

The whispers curled around Susanna. Hopes and wishes were inhaled with each breath.

Padre Giovanni, the priest who said Mass and listened from his confessional to the girls' deepest secrets, lifted the goblet of wine toward the big cross where Jesus hung. He prayed— *"Dominus vobiscum . . ."*—as he performed the transubstantiation.

It was a mystery, a miracle, the way the clear red wine became Jesus's blood, the way the thin wafers became his body.

But today Susanna didn't care about the miracles of the wine and bread. She cared about the miracle of the visitors who'd come. Were they really here to *adopt*?

Susanna sighed. She already knew she wouldn't

be one of the girls chosen to leave. She looked down at her hands. When the girls were being nice, they said she was the color of *cappuccino*. When they were mean, they said her skin was the color of unwashed brown potatoes.

Suor Vicenza stood with her conductor's baton to lead them in the next hymn. The youngest nun, she had a sweet round face. With an upward arc, she lifted her gentle arm to lead the singing.

Pina might be chosen for adoption. Pina, Susanna's pretty best friend. Pina with her milk-white skin, her gleaming yellow hair, braided and wound over her head like a crown.

Susanna loved to play hairdresser with Pina's blond hair, while Pina struggled to do the same with Susanna's wiry curls.

The nuns said that as babies, they'd sat next to each other and rocked back and forth in the high chairs placed at the edges of the dining room. Later they'd played rag dolls. Summers, they'd hidden from each other behind the pots of tomato plants and dwarf lemon trees on the rooftop *terrazzo*.

Whereas Pina believed herself to be an orphan, Carla, on the other side of her, had parents. Every month they came to see her. After the visits, Carla bit her fingernails a little deeper, gnawing on them, exposing the raw places.

One time, Susanna had asked, "Carla, why don't you live with your parents?"

Carla had lifted up her head, pointing her long nose in the air, and said, "My parents are important, and they live in a far-off country and can only visit me sometimes on business trips."

Someone had snickered.

"They're too important for *her*," someone else had whispered.

Susanna herself had seen Carla's *papà* hand bundles of *lire* to Suor Anna.

And she'd heard Carla crying in the night.

It would serve her parents right if she got adopted!

Maybe Donatella, standing in front of Susanna, would go. Donatella liked to brag that she was half American. But that was why she was there at the *Istituto*. The whisperers said that Donatella's mother had been the girlfriend of an American GI, a liberator of Italy from the Fascist dogs. Maybe, in the fierce fight, he'd gotten killed. Or maybe he'd run away once his girlfriend became a mother. And now Donatella's mother, said those whisperers, was married to another man. A man who didn't know about the liberator or his child. Donatella was a secret, hidden away there. At the *Istituto di Gesù Bambino.*

Maybe it would be Elvira. On Sundays, Elvira wore her hair, the color of that fox fur on the visitor's coat, tied with a special blue ribbon.

When Elvira's grandmother visited, blue-ribboned Elvira slipped into the *stanza della compagnia* to meet her. But so far, her *nonna* had brought not an invitation to a beautiful new life but only chocolates.

The twins, Antonetta and Georgina, identical with their crisp black curls and their green cat eyes, were true orphans. But at least they had each other. Would the looking couples want to get two new daughters at the same time? Wouldn't that be too much?

No matter what, Susanna repeated to herself, she would not be the one.

"You're a *mulatta*," Suor Anna had once said. "A cross between a white person and a black one. I can tell by your tight curls, your dark skin. Surely, your father was an American soldier. A *nero*. No Italians have hair or skin like yours."

Susanna had never seen a *nero*. She'd only read about them in the book of Robinson Crusoe. In that story, all the *neri* had been cannibals. She shivered at the thought of people eating people.

"Cannibale," the girls sometimes called Susanna.

Italian parents would want a girl with creamy skin and hair that could be stroked with a brush one hundred times at night. A daughter who looked like them. They wouldn't want a half-cannibal daughter.

She wouldn't implore. With her head held high, Susanna focused on Jesus hanging on the cross, his throbbing, pulsing heart exposed for everyone to see.

A Beautiful Smile

PINA SNIFFED THE SMELL of the thick pizza squares layered with tomatoes and the rubbery yellow cheese the American soldiers had left behind when they marched out of Italy. The fragrant odors came right into the *chiesa*.

She loved Sunday pizza, baked in the big oven, but today there was something even more pressing: rumor had it that the strangers had come to take someone to a new home.

Pina pictured the fat woman's house, big like she was, with a room just for a daughter. The fat woman might sew her daughter a dress with tiny pink rosebuds, with fine white ribbons that curled up on the ends. Every day she and her daughter would drink hot chocolate and eat flaky, sugary *sfogliatelle*.

Pina imagined snuggling against the woman's big body at night. The bed would be covered with a goose-down blanket, fluffy as a summer thunderhead. For once, in winter she'd be warm.

After Mass, Pina ran ahead of the others and surveyed the dining room. Could she sit close to one of those mothers or fathers? There—the short woman with the red fur on her coat had an empty place in front of her.

As she crossed the room, Pina undid the crown of her blond braids and flipped them so they hung down her back. She seated herself on the bench across from the short woman.

Short Woman's husband was at the other end of the table. The nuns must have spread the strangers out so that everyone would have a chance to meet them.

The short woman looked at Pina and smiled. Pina passed her a tray of pizza. The woman eased a piece onto her plate. She picked up the pizza, then put it back down. She picked it up and took a bite. She put it down. She smiled.

Pina smiled back. As hungry as she was—tummy rumbling—she wouldn't eat. She needed to concentrate. She tucked her napkin neatly around her neck. As a daughter, she would be no trouble. She would not be messy. She would be cheerful all the time.

"Why, you have a beautiful smile," said Short Woman, and Pina smiled harder. "What is your name, dear?"

"Giuseppina." Pina showed her white teeth. "I am called Pina."

So far, all was going well. Maybe soon she would be taken to the visiting room off the church—the *stanza della compagnia*—where this woman and her short husband would get to know her better.

Just then, Pina looked up to see Suor Anna frowning at the short woman. Sorella was shaking her head a little. Just a little. The woman wrinkled her smooth, white forehead.

Pina stared up at Suor Anna. She didn't understand. Was Sorella shaking her head because Pina stole candies, forcing her hand into the narrow neck of the jar? Because she flicked water at the kitchen cat? Talked back to the nuns? Was Sorella warning the woman off, telling her that Pina would not make a good daughter?

The woman smiled at Pina one more time. She dropped her eyes and fiddled with her napkin. Then she picked up her pizza again and turned to Elvira with her fiery hair. "What a beautiful color. . . ."

Pina dabbed at her eyes with her napkin. She pushed her pizza aside. What had she done?

Right before the Sunday afternoon bingo game, Pina slipped into the classroom. She took paper and a pencil from the teacher's desk and made a portrait of Suor Anna. She bore down hard as she drew Sorella's face skinnier than it really was, wrinklier than it really was, the small eyes even smaller. Then she put the paper, unfolded, into the bowl of bingo chips from which Suor Anna would draw.

Pina left the classroom and, when the rest of the girls entered, mingled innocently with them.

Of course, Suor Anna pulled out the drawing right away. As she stared at it, Pina pretended to be interested in her blank bingo card.

If Suor Anna found her out, Pina would be punished by the meanest nun, Suor Rosa. Suor Rosa, her face alive with pulsing red veins, was in charge of discipline. If Suor Rosa learned that Pina had drawn such a hateful portrait of Suor Anna, she might lock Pina in a dark closet or strike her with the stick used to beat the dust from mattresses.

Pina studied the bare classroom walls, which had once been white but were now yellowed, the plaster brittle and cracked. A lone crucifix hung at the front of the room.

Sorella turned the unflattering portrait so it faced the class. "Which of you did this?"

The girls stared. Pina stared too, as though she knew nothing. She heard muffled giggles. From behind, Susanna gave her a poke in the back.

When Sorella looked over the room, her eyes, Pina felt, rested longest on her.

Wings

THE FOLLOWING SUNDAY, Susanna gestured toward the man and woman nicknamed Fat with Thin. "That couple is going to adopt Fiorentina after Mass today."

"How do you know?" Pina asked.

"Fiorentina told me."

Standing on the wooden steps, waiting to sing, Susanna watched Fiorentina. Fiorentina's large eyes darted to the couple that sat in the front row—the woman now wearing a dress with narrow stripes, her thin husband wearing the same brown suit as before.

Susanna ran her eyes over the other couples in the *chiesa*. The pair that caught her attention was a young blond woman with a gray-headed man. Might the man be the woman's husband, or her father?

Just as Mass was about to begin, Suor Anna approached the steps, beckoning to Fiorentina with her long, crooked finger.

Susanna watched Fiorentina make her way among the girls, down the steps.

Sorella led her by the hand to the front pew where Fat with Thin sat. The couple smiled shyly. When Sorella leaned over to say something, they scooted apart so that Fiorentina could sit between them. Fiorentina stumbled as she made her way to her new place. And throughout Mass, she sat stiffly, hands folded her in lap, eyes still darting.

As though nothing unusual was going on, Suor Vicenza lifted her baton to lead the singing.

Suor Vicenza had recently undergone a ceremony, transforming herself from an *aspirante* to a *postulante,* a beginner nun. The girls had stared with wide eyes as she'd floated down the aisle of the *chiesa* dressed in a lacy white bridal gown, preparing to be a Bride of Christ. Afterward the nuns had cut off her pretty hair and she wore the black nun habit.

At the end of Mass, Suor Anna stood, saying, "Come make your good-byes to Fiorentina, girls. She's going with her parents today."

Fiorentina stood by the confessional while the girls crowded around.

"Write to us!"

"Tell us how it is."

"Don't forget us!"

Fiorentina brushed back tears.

Susanna hugged Fiorentina, feeling her thin shoulder blades. They were like wings ready to fly away.

When she let go—saying, "Goodbye, Fiorentina. Be happy!"—Susanna herself felt completely earthbound, flying nowhere, stuck here.

"That's enough, girls," Suor Anna declared. "Time to let Fiorentina go. Perhaps she'll visit us soon."

Fiorentina took her place between her parents, smiling, her tears now dry.

After they left, everyone rushed to the windows to look down at the street.

"They'll come out soon."

"Seven flights takes a while."

Soon the trio emerged, tiny as dolls below. They could have been dolls, Susanna thought; the scene felt so unreal. Fiorentina walked with her new mother on one side, her father on the other.

They all three got into a nice black car. The engine sputtered, and the car drove away.

As the other girls left for Sunday lunch, Susanna and Pina stayed behind, looking down at the street filled with honking cars.

"I wasn't that close to Fiorentina," Susanna said slowly, "but I'll miss her."

"Where do you think she's gone?" asked Pina, edging closer to Susanna.

"To a restaurant to eat shrimp and veal and lobster."

Pina laughed. "They'll have *spumoni* for dessert."

"And then they'll go to the dressmaker's to get new clothes."

"Clothes that aren't black."

"Cashmere," pronounced Susanna.

"Or silk."

But it wasn't those things Susanna wanted. She wanted someone to love her for who she was. She wanted a parent to come looking for a dark child. Only a dark parent would want her. The people of Naples were browner than those of the north, but no Italian had skin as dark as hers.

Going into the dining room, Susanna watched

Pina glance around for a spot close to one of the looking couples.

"Fiorentina went. Maybe I have a chance," Pina said. "I'd make a good blond daughter for that blond lady."

"But then you'd have that old father."

"Better than none. Maybe he'd be my grand-father."

Grandfather, Susanna thought. Families came with a whole cast of relatives—grandfather, grand-mother, uncle, and aunt—not just father and mother.

Maybe she should sit close to someone too. But she and Pina had come in late, and the benches were already full of other girls smiling and flirting.

The room was fragrant with the smell of hot pizza, of basil and oregano.

"I really need to be adopted," Pina said, taking a square of pizza onto her plate. "Unlike some of the others, I don't have a family. I'm sure that my parents were both war heroes. I'm sure that they're both dead."

Susanna lifted her pizza carefully to her mouth. She and Pina had talked like this many times, as though saying the words made them true. "Maybe mine are dead too. If our parents weren't dead, they would have come."

She'd heard from the nuns that as a baby she'd been left in a basket on the doorstep of the *Istituto*. Who had left her? And why? Had they abandoned her because she was a *mulatta*? Tainted with *nero* blood?

Susanna took Pina's arm. "We'll just stay here together."

"Or go together," Pina said.

"What do you think of the parents here today?" Susanna asked, looking around.

"They're not interested in me," Pina said. "They don't even give me a chance. I told you how Suor Anna shook her head at that short woman who liked me last Sunday. Now no one cares. Suor Anna must talk to people before they even see me."

"Maybe she does. You're so pretty, you'd think they'd at least smile at you. Because I'm a *mulatta*, I'll have to live at the *Istituto* forever. Maybe I'll become a nun."

Pina rolled her eyes. "Not *that*."

"We could become nuns together."

Pina banged the table.

"I was only joking," Susanna said. She had often imagined that she and Pina were sisters, *sorelle,* but not *that* kind—not sisters in service of Jesus—*real* sisters. Family.

Susanna wished again that she had light skin like the other girls and hair that didn't snarl up like a scrub brush. She was glad there were no mirrors at the *Istituto.* Seeing what she already did of her brown body, feeling her impossible hair, was enough.

Pina, on the other hand, stared at her reflection in the window glass. She combed her yellow hair, turning this way and that for better views.

Whenever Suor Rosa caught Pina at this, she pulled the curtains, saying, "That's vanity, Giuseppina."

Once Pina had rolled her hair around pieces of string and tied the ends to make curls. At breakfast, seeing her hair, Suor Rosa had ordered: "Go wet your hair, Giuseppina."

The next afternoon, Maestra Artura was reading an Italian poem about a fish market. She and her sister, Maestra Adrianna, had been sent by the city of Naples to teach the girls at the *Istituto.* Unlike the nuns, who wore long, voluminous habits, the teachers wore tight, short skirts. When they sat down, their chubby legs slightly spread, their underwear showed.

Susanna gazed at the gray sky outside, at the rain dripping from the building opposite, where a yellow light was on in a flat. A woman was tending a pot on the stove. The room was painted a rusty red.

One time, peering across at the neighboring building, she and Pina had seen a couple kissing in a tenth-floor apartment. They'd been trying to see such a delicious sight ever since.

Maestra Artura closed the book of poetry, leaving them with the image of women carrying large earthenware jars of olives on their heads. Susanna imagined balancing such a heavy burden.

"Today is the first day of Advent, girls," she said. "Before you leave today, please write your letters to *La Befana*. Tell her what you want."

La Befana, the angel who dressed like a witch, would hide presents in the middle of the night before Three Kings' Day, January sixth.

Pens scratched as the girls wrote.

Pina held up hers for Susanna to read.

Cara Befana,

I'm sorry if I have been bad. I will be good. I won't talk back to the nuns. I won't tell lies. I won't steal candy.

Please grant all my wishes. I want some cannoli *and* sfogliatelle. *Some* gelato *would be nice too.*

When Susanna stopped reading, Pina said, "Do I dare ask for what I really want?"

"What do you mean?"

"For parents to adopt me."

Susanna snorted. "That's crazy, Pina. *La Befana* can't bring you things like that."

"Who says?"

"All she ever brings is games and clothes, no matter what."

"Well, I can at least *try*." Pina turned away and bent to her paper.

Elvira looked up from her letter, saying, "Just because you're a *mulatta* and there's no hope for *you*, Susanna, doesn't mean that *La Befana* won't find a family for Pina."

"No angel will get any of you parents," Susanna said quietly.

She decided not to write to *La Befana*. She was certain that, as she did every year, *La Befana* would bring only dominoes and underwear, *biscotti* and mints. Or coal and garlic if a girl was really bad.

There was no chance of her bringing parents.

The girls finished their letters and, in small groups, went to the *chiesa*. Susanna pictured them tucking their letters into the straw of the Nativity, right under Jesus's crib, next to the plaster animals. The crib would still be empty. The nuns would put the Jesus statue into the crib on the night before Christmas.

As Pina left the classroom, she caught Susanna's eye, held up the letter, and pointed to the sentence she'd added.

Coal and Garlic

ALL DURING MASS AND THE BREAKFAST of bread and oranges, Pina could hardly sit still. It was January sixth, the day of hunting for *La Befana*'s presents.

Pina's new family wasn't hidden here—she knew that—but she would search for a sign. Maybe a letter.

She finished her wedge of orange, biting the flesh down to the white of the skin.

The girls carried their plates into the kitchen. Finally, they all stood in line to use the bathroom.

"Hurry up!" Pina said to Georgina, ahead of her.

Finally, Suor Anna gave the signal with her bony finger.

The building was filled with shouts and cries as everyone hunted.

Pina looked in the dust under her bunk, in the huge pizza oven with its creaking hinges, behind the droopy gray curtains covering the hallway windows.

Maybe her new mother would wear a blue dress and high heels, a small purse tucked under her arm. She imagined a father with light hair and green eyes. He'd wear a suit with wide lapels. He'd put his hands in his trouser pockets, jingling change.

And they would take her shopping for a white dress with rosebuds made of ribbon, a silky fur coat. In the house, there would be tiny glass animals and bowls of chocolate truffles and tulips fresh from the florist. Maybe she'd even have her own pony.

But she found nothing.

"*La Befana* forgot me!" she cried to Suor Rosa, whose spidery red veins crisscrossed her cheeks.

"Were you good or bad?" Suor asked.

Pina hung her head.

"Look under the skirt of the altar."

Pina ran into the *chiesa* and up the steps to the altar. She lifted the satin. Yes! There was a package. It had her name written in big letters: GIUSEPPINA.

The package was too round to be a letter. But one never knew. Pina tore off the wrapping.

There lay a lump of coal and a clove of garlic.

She crumpled the paper with the coal and garlic inside and threw it. It landed near the feet of the statue of the Virgin. Pina wiped her black, smelly hands on the satin skirt of the altar. She slumped down, her face in her hands.

She heard footsteps but didn't look up. Then she heard Suor Vicenza's sweet voice above her.

"Don't cry, Pina. Talk to Jesus instead," Suor Vicenza said. "Promise to be good. Maybe Jesus will send you something." She helped Pina up, and together they walked to a pew.

While Sorella knelt beside her, Pina prayed, fingering her white glass rosary. "I promise. I promise . . ." She tried to love Jesus instead of hating that old witch, *La Befana.*

"So cruel . . ." she heard Sorella mutter.

Pina tried to pray in earnest, but if she didn't hurry, all the gifts would be found. Maybe even the letter meant for her. Another girl would be adopted in her place.

She looked over at Suor Vicenza.

"Look in the towel cabinet," whispered Sorella.

Could a letter be hidden in the *towel cabinet*? The letter from her new family?

With a final "I promise you, Jesus!" Pina thrust her rosary into her pocket and rushed out of the *chiesa*. As she passed the pews and kneelers, she glanced to see if anything was still hidden there.

Under the pile of frayed white towels, there was a package with no name. It too was roundish. Not a letter. As Pina tore the package open, black socks and an orange tumbled out. She picked up the socks and squeezed them hard in her fist. She wrung them between both hands. How she hated these socks! And she'd already eaten an orange at breakfast!

She plunged her fingernail into the orange peel, pulling back the bright skin. The bitter oil burned the tender place under her nail.

How she hated everyone! Even Suor Vicenza!

She noticed a group of girls gathered around Carla. Whatever Carla was saying was even more interesting than hunting for *La Befana*'s gifts. Maybe *she'd* gotten a letter, a sign. . . .

"Elvira and I stayed up last night," Carla was

A Letter

SUSANNA PULLED DOWN THE CUFFS of her black sweater. If Suor Anna had called her into her office, it had to be about something important. She studied the crucifix, and from there her eyes moved to the large crack that ran along the wall.

Suor Anna sat with her old white hands folded on the desk. "Susanna," she began, then paused. "Susanna," she started again, "I've received a letter from someone who says he may be your father."

The room got brighter, then dimmer. Susanna heard the soft tick of Suor Anna's wristwatch. She gripped the arms of her chair.

Finally, she said, "My *father*?" Floating into the cold room, the word sounded odd, as if from a foreign language.

"Apparently so." Sorella looked down into her folded hands.

"Is he coming here?" Susanna asked. She wanted to add *to get me* but didn't dare. His very existence was fragile enough.

"He has what's called a tour of duty and won't come for a little while."

A little while would give her a chance to get used to the idea. Susanna wished she could see the letter from this man. Her father. She glanced at Suor Anna's bare desk.

Sorella unfolded her hands and folded them again, the fingers laced tightly. "He's an American sailor," she said, then paused. "He's sure to be dark skinned."

"I know," Susanna said softly, her heart beating happily. The surprise was that he was a sailor, not a *soldier*, as she'd imagined.

Was he really coming for *her*? Would he love her enough to take her with him? Was she good enough? Would he really want her? She stared down at her hands, the color of unwashed potatoes.

"What is my father's name?" Susanna asked.

"James Green."

James Green, Susanna repeated silently to herself.

Pina would feel terrible, she suddenly thought.

"It's important for you to keep in mind, Susanna, that this man may not be your father. It isn't certain."

"How will it become certain?"

Sorella twisted her gold wedding band, her Bride-of-Christ ring, on her bony finger. "Perhaps you and he will look alike."

Susanna wondered who would be the judge of that. It would be hard to come close yet not know for sure—to have this father go away.

"What about my mother?"

Around and around went Sorella's ring. "He did write about that too. He . . . he . . . said she's passed on."

Susanna gripped the arms of the chair again. Although she and Pina had always talked as though their mothers were dead, the truth sent a chill through her. A black chasm had opened. Susanna realized that deep down she'd always held on to the tiny hope that she had a mother.

"I will let you know," Sorella said gently, "when I hear from your father again."

"Yes, Sorella." Susanna stood. As she stepped into the hall, she realized she was not the same person who'd entered the office. She'd been an orphan then. Now, moments later, she was a daughter. *Maybe* a daughter, she corrected herself.

Susanna found Pina reading a comic book about two sheep. The sheep teased a gray wolf who was always trying to eat them. She sat down beside her. "I was in Suor Anna's office just now. She had news for me."

Pina set the comic book aside. On the cover the three animals smiled, their paws and hooves lifted. "Good news? Or bad?"

"Good, I guess. My father may have found me."

A silence fell between them. It was like a heavy stone falling into the lake at the Bosco dei Tre Mari.

Pina ruffled the pages of the comic book.

"But he's not taking me away yet," Susanna said slowly. "He's not even coming to see me for a while." She felt like smiling and lifting her hand like the sheep and wolf. "He may not come at all."

She wished she could say, *I'll take you with me. We'll be sisters.* But she didn't know if she herself would go anywhere.

Pina opened the comic book. She ran her eyes over the pages and turned them, as though she were really reading.

At least, Susanna thought, she could ease Pina's hurt a little. "Sorella had bad news for me too. My mother's dead."

"But you *knew* that," Pina said without looking up.

That night, Susanna stared up at Pina's bunk above her. The world had spread open for her, beyond the walls of the *Istituto*. It had suddenly expanded as far as America. Susanna searched her memory for an image of the map of the Western Hemisphere. She pictured the boot-shaped country of Italy, the protected womb of the Mediterranean Sea, and then the wide abyss of ocean that stood between Europe and America. At the entry to America, the Statue of Liberty greeted everyone with a welcoming flame.

She imagined crossing the ocean to America on a large ship, rocking across the water, standing with her father as drops of salty water blew against their faces.

Then a new thought, like a lump under the bedsheet, caused her to turn over, to bury her face in the pillow. Her father had left her here for all these years. And why didn't he give up *everything* to rush to her now? What was a tour of duty, after all, compared to a daughter? Why the wait?

Nonetheless, when he did come, *if* he came, she would throw herself into his arms. She would unite herself with him. They would never be separated again.

Ave Maria

WEARING HER BLACK CAPE and black beret, Pina
got in line behind Carla in the hallway.

"Where are we going?" she whispered.

Carla shrugged. "The nuns didn't say."

At least they were going *out*. Pina always liked
to leave the *Istituto*.

Suor Anna swung open the big door, and the
line moved down the flights of marble steps. The
centers of the steps were worn from people walking up and down. At each landing, the line made
a sharp turn and Pina looked up at the rest of the
girls still descending. The pounding of their footsteps echoed upward.

Seven landings, seven flights of steps, and they
passed through the archway and into the street.

The building was as gray as the sky and
stretched from one street to the next. Pina counted

the floors—the *Istituto* was on the seventh, and there were three more above and, finally, the roof garden. The bare branches of fig trees poked up from the top wall.

When everyone was in line on the sidewalk, Suor Rosa said, "Keep your eyes on the ground, girls."

Beyond the sidewalk crowded with people in a hurry, peddlers wheeling small carts, and a man strolling with an accordion, the cars blared their horns.

The nuns got into place beside the line, in front of it, and behind it. Suor Rosa pushed Pina's head down, her hand firm on the back of her neck. "Don't look around, Giuseppina."

Yet Pina peeked anyway to see a woman lowering a basket on a rope from a window. Below, a man filled the basket with long loaves of bread, and the woman jerked the basket back up.

She saw a group of street urchins throwing stones at a brightly painted gypsy wagon.

The nuns led the way down one alley, then another. They walked over the underground tunnels, where people had lived during the bombing. They'd set up entire villages underground, shuddering together at the explosions.

Bright laundry hung from the balconies, fluttering in the cold wind. Two women carried on a conversation, shouting from one balcony to the other.

Where were they going? Pina wondered. This didn't seem like a field trip.

They climbed a steep hill, and the volcano, Vesuvio, appeared. The snow on top was like a white shawl around a woman's shoulders.

The volcano had last erupted as the war was ending. Although Pina had been a baby and didn't remember the eruption, she'd heard stories of the black cloud that had unfurled from the mountain, the rain of hot ash and cinders, the frightening way the earth had rocked. Now Pina always studied Vesuvio for signs of smoke.

The line stopped. Suor Anna looked at a piece of paper in her hand and then at a building, then back at the paper. She led the line into a courtyard with a pointy cypress tree, the brown needles lying in a pile at the base of the trunk.

The girls marched up four flights of steps, their black shoes pounding.

Sorella held up her paper again, then knocked at a door.

Pina stood on tiptoe and saw the door opened by a man with a pink carnation in his buttonhole. The man swung the door wide open.

Inside the apartment, they crossed a white marble floor with gray veins like small rivers. The girls took off their berets and held them in front of them.

As the man led them into a big room with a tall ceiling, people dressed in black clothes crowded in front of a painting of the Virgin.

Pina sniffed. The room smelled like the water in vases of rotten flowers. Like old Friday *baccalà* fish soup. Like a toilet that hadn't been flushed. She wanted to hold her nose.

Suor Rosa pushed her sharp finger between Pina's shoulder blades, urging her closer. "Go on, Giuseppina," she whispered. "Gaze on the beautiful face."

The people dressed in black shuffled away, and the girls gathered in. Pina looked into the box.

Inside the box lay a little girl, her blond hair against the lacy pillow. A blue glass rosary was draped across her white dress, and her small hands clutched the rosary's cross.

"She looks like you, Pina," whispered Donatella.

Mother of God! Pina felt for her own rosary in her pocket. She wrapped her fingers around it, warming the cold beads.

As they each stepped forward, the room quieted. The clock ticked; a man coughed.

The death smell mixed with the sweet lily smell.

"Ave Maria," Suor Rosa began, and all the relatives cried at once. A loud crying that ran like a river, filling the room, almost drowning everyone. Sorella's face was so red from cold that the red lines barely showed.

Pina's legs cramped from standing, and her toes bumped the ends of her black shoes. The smell made her stomach flip like a caught fish.

Halfway into the second Rosary, Pina found herself looking into the eyes of the *mammina* standing by the coffin, black lace tied over her round head. She had a sudden thought, a thought that made her forget to be afraid: Did this poor, sad family need a new child to replace that one lying there? Might she, Pina, be that new child?

It was more important than ever to get a family, now that Susanna's father was on the way to get her.

The Rosaries ended.

"Girls," said Suor Rosa, "you are here to sing hymns for the dead. Please begin."

Suor Vicenza pulled the conductor's baton from the sleeve of her habit. She lifted it, and began to lead the *Ave Maria*.

Pina smiled and sang loudly. She even cried a little and lifted her face to show tears. She knew from studying herself in the window glass that she looked even prettier when she suffered.

But that *mamma* was too *triste* to care about an orphan. She just sobbed into her balled-up handkerchief.

At the end, the man with the carnation counted many *lire* into Suor Anna's open hands, saying, "They have lovely voices."

Suor Vicenza frowned and whispered to Suor Anna.

Loudly, Suor Anna said, "However else will we get money to feed them?"

In the following weeks, the nuns took the girls all over Naples to sing for the dead—from the villas on the hillsides of Il Vomero to the dirty alleys in the south. At each funeral, someone gave the nuns money for the singing.

"We walk too much!" Pina complained to Susanna. "The nuns should use some of the funeral money to buy us new shoes!" She held up her black ones, holes worn in the soles.

One cold, sunny morning, they walked in a funeral procession for a dead dairyman, and for weeks metal containers of real milk arrived, thick and creamy. No powdered American soldier milk for a while! When the nuns scooped the cream off the top and spread it on *panini,* Pina gobbled it down, licking her fingers.

At every funeral, she thought of the dead girl in the coffin. That mother had cried over her daughter, had cried so hard that she hadn't even seen beautiful Pina.

Pina needed a *mamma* to cry over *her* that way. So far, she wasn't having any luck. She needed help—if not from *La Befana,* then from the Virgin Mary. People prayed the Rosary to Mary, asking for blessings. But the Virgin especially loved those who went beyond prayer. Mary loved those who suffered. Could she suffer in a special way, Pina wondered, and thus catch the attention of the Blessed Virgin?

Black Yarn

ONE AFTERNOON when school was over and Susanna was clearing off her desk for dominoes, when Maestra Adrianna and Maestra Artura were packing their purses and pulling up their stockings, Suor Vicenza entered the classroom. "Put away the dominoes, girls." She placed two baskets on the teachers' desk: one large, one smaller. "You have something new to learn today."

With the side of her hand, Susanna slid the dominoes into the box and closed the lid. "What could it be?" she whispered to Pina.

"Work of some kind," Pina said.

When the clatter of dominoes had died away, Sorella carried around the small basket. "These are crochet hooks," she explained. "Each of you please take one."

"It's a tiny shepherd's staff," joked Pina as she lifted out a metal tool.

Then Suor Vicenza passed the large basket. It contained balls of black yarn.

Susanna held the soft globe in both hands.

Pina's rolled off the desk, unraveling.

When each girl had taken yarn, Sorella held her hook high in the air and, with great exaggerated gestures, tied the wool onto it. "Today you will learn to crochet. We will start with a chain." She showed how to loop the yarn around the hook, how to pull it through. "Now you try. Keep hooking and looping."

The girls began to work as Sorella made the rounds, leaning close, gently guiding.

As Susanna crocheted, she thought of the man who claimed he was her father. Weeks had passed, and there'd been no further word from him. Every day, Susanna had looked into Suor Anna's narrow white face for a sign. But none came. It was as though Susanna's visit to the office had never taken place. Was he still on that tour of duty?

As she hooked the yarn and looped it, Susanna felt small knots form inside her. Why would a father not drop everything to hurry to his daughter?

Susanna completed the stitches, and her chain grew longer. She imagined herself casting this chain into the world to reel her *papà* in. Once she'd captured him, she'd link the two of them together with this length of soft blackness. As her fingers memorized the small, precise movements and her mind was freed, Susanna again tried to picture this father. No images came to mind. Only a feeling of being enfolded. Of being protected at last, taken in.

As Suor Vicenza bent close, Susanna smelled the laundry soap of her black and white habit. The yarn chain already reached the floor.

"Very nice, Susanna. You're learning quickly." Sorella touched the wool with her fingertip, her nail neat and short. "Just make the loops more even."

Very nice. On her first try. Susanna looped the yarn carefully over the hook. From now on, she'd create perfect loops. Someday her father would see her crocheting. He'd have to love her for being so clever.

"Now you will crochet your own black berets," Suor Vicenza announced.

She showed how to link the chain to make a circle.

"From now on, you won't need anyone to buy

these for you," she said as the circles of the berets grew bigger.

"The nuns are saving money again," remarked Pina.

As Susanna crocheted, she thought of how, soon, she'd know enough to make her father a sweater. Maybe socks. Or warm mittens. She wouldn't use dreary black yarn, but red, yellow, green—all the colors of happiness.

Corn Husks

PINA JUMPED FROM ONE BIG YELLOW flower on the carpet to the next. "Follow me!" she called to Susanna.

"Pina!" called Suor Rosa. "Behave yourself! This is a public theater!"

Pina slowed down. She didn't want to get punished, didn't want to miss seeing the movie, *The Miracle of Our Lady of Fatima.*

"See, Pina?" said Susanna. "The funeral money gets spent on a good cause. The nuns have paid for us to come here."

"I think they got the tickets for free," countered Pina as they entered the dark theater.

"How about here?" Susanna asked, pointing at two seats in the middle.

"I want to go right up front," answered Pina, leading the way. She didn't mind craning her neck.

As the movie was about to start, the curtain slowly rose, revealing the screen. This was Pina's favorite moment. "Shhh," she said to Elvira and Carla, who giggled and unwrapped candies.

The lights went down, the projector rolled, and the movie flashed onto the screen.

The black-and-white vision of the Virgin Mary was huge and so lovely that Pina sucked in her breath. It was as though she herself knelt in awe alongside the two shepherd girls in the field.

From a cloud, the Virgin pronounced that the girls would have to endure much suffering.

"We will pray the Rosary every day," the girls promised.

"Me too," Pina whispered to Susanna. Her neck was beginning to ache.

One of the girls had a mean mother, who tried to keep her daughter from going to see the Virgin. Each time that Lucia had to choose between her own *mamma* and the Holy Mother, Pina's heart twisted. What suffering the Virgin demanded, making a girl choose like that!

Pina thought she'd rather be Lucia and have a mean mother than none at all. And yet could she, any more than Lucia, choose her own mother over the Mother of All, the Blessed Virgin?

She put this dilemma out of her mind and thought of something else. The movie was about miracles, and she surely needed one. But how? She rubbed her neck with her fingertips.

"If I can just see the Holy Mother, maybe someone will make a movie about *me*," Pina whispered to Susanna. "Someone will watch it and see that I'm special. That person will adopt me."

"That's just a dream," said Susanna.

"You never dream," argued Pina. "If I don't dream, my dreams will never come true."

"They don't anyway."

"I'll have to suffer to see the Virgin. . . ." said Pina.

"Shut up and watch the movie," someone said.

That night Pina crawled into Susanna's bunk with her. "I want to suffer," she whispered.

"What kind of suffering?"

"I'm trying to think."

"They put nails in Jesus's hands and feet," Susanna mused. "The saints suffered—Joan of

Arc was burned at the stake; Saint Stephen was shot full of arrows. . . ."

"I don't want to suffer *that* much," Pina said. She grew silent, imagining the terrible torture of nails, fire, and arrows. Would the Virgin truly ask that much? Pina turned her mind to lesser sufferings. Finally, she thought of something.

While Susanna dozed, breathing softly beside her, Pina worked through the details of her plan. When she was sure everyone was sleeping, she shook Susanna gently. "Let's go."

"Go where?" Susanna murmured.

"To the rooftop. Remember the suffering?"

Pina swung her legs out of bed, her feet on the cold tiles.

Slowly Susanna rose and sat beside her. "Is this another of your wild ideas?"

"Of course not. This idea will work," Pina whispered. She led the way down the dormitory of sleeping girls. Out in the hallway, Pina paused to listen at the door of the nuns' dormitory. All was hushed.

They moved past the *chiesa* and the *stanza della compagnia.*

By the big oven, the kitchen cat stared with his yellow eyes, poised to lunge at the rats.

Pina reached for Susanna's hand.

"Meow," said Susanna, and they giggled.

At the big door leading out, they paused again. Listened. No one. They climbed flight after flight of stairs until they reached the *terrazzo*.

In the moonlit night, the apartments in the nearby buildings had their lamps on. A breeze blew the corn husks drying on the line, rattling them. The nuns used the husks for weaving baskets to sell.

By the moonlight, Pina unclipped several husks. She tied them together, end to end, making a cord.

Pina lifted up her nightdress, held the hem between her teeth, and wrapped the cord around her waist. She tied it tightly.

"What are you *doing*, Pina?" Susanna leaned forward in the moonlight.

"I'm going to suffer. This is so scratchy, so itchy. It's perfect."

Courage

SUSANNA WAITED FOR PINA outside the bathroom stall. What was taking her so long?

When Pina came out, she had tears in her eyes. "I pulled the cord tighter," she whispered to Susanna. "Every day it burns more."

"You're crazy," Susanna said. "You should take that thing off."

"A miracle takes courage. I have to suffer."

Susanna worried about her friend. Lately Pina knelt for long periods, staring into the air, fingering her rosary. Sometimes she crossed her eyes as though looking for something that wasn't there.

As Susanna washed her face, Pina said, "This morning, I thought I saw the outline of the Virgin."

"Hmm."

"Should I tell Padre Giovanni?"

"Not until you're sure, Pina. You're starting to smell funny." Susanna wrinkled her nose.

Yet as Susanna ran her damp fingers through her hair, she thought of how her own *papà* hadn't come, even though she waited so eagerly. Might it take a miracle to summon him? Should she try to suffer the way Pina did? Was Pina doing the right thing?

Hot, Bitter
Pomegranate Juice

"YOUR FACE IS FLUSHED, PINA," said Suor Vicenza at breakfast. "Let me take your temperature." She led Pina away from her bowl of figs and bread to the sickroom.

Sorella shook the silver mercury down in the thermometer, then put the thermometer under Pina's tongue. Sorella looked at her watch. Then she slipped the thermometer out, held it to the light, and sighed. "You have a fever, Pina. Lie down."

When Suor Vicenza laid a cool hand on Pina's forehead, Pina shuddered. Sorella put an extra blanket around her. She brought her a cup of hot, bitter pomegranate juice.

Soon a man with a huge mustache came to the side of her bed. He carried a black suitcase and smelled of spicy pipe tobacco.

"This is Dr. Calvino, Pina," Suor Vicenza said gently. "He is here to cure you."

The doctor sat down on the bed. He felt Pina's forehead with his own cool hand. He loosened her clothes until he found the rotting corn husks. A horrible smell drifted into the room. "What have you done, Giuseppina? What is this you've done?" The doctor's voice grew loud: "You have an infection. Why did you do a thing like this?" He held up the remains of a corn husk.

Pina squeezed her eyes shut.

"Why did you do this thing?" Dr. Calvino asked again.

"I wanted to suffer," Pina said in a small voice. "I wanted someone to adopt me. I wanted to see the Virgin Mary."

"You wanted *what*?" the doctor asked, his eyebrows pinching together. "How does tying a rope around your waist help you see the Blessed Mother? How does infecting yourself get you a home?"

Pina began to sob.

"Don't cry, Pina. That will make you feel worse," said Suor Vicenza.

The doctor spoke again, this time more softly.

"People only want to adopt healthy girls, Giuseppina. Promise me you won't do such a foolish thing again."

Pina covered her face, looking for the image of the Virgin in the blackness.

The Telegram

TWO DAYS LATER, when Susanna was coming out of the dormitory, light from the window casting a golden patch on the black-and-white tiles, she heard voices in the hallway.

"You'd think she'd come when Giuseppina is so sick," Suor Anna said. "She might even die. She's her mother, after all."

Susanna bent to buckle her shoe, holding her breath so she wouldn't miss a word.

The nuns drew nearer, their black habits swishing, the rosary beads that hung from their waists clicking. "Maybe the telegram didn't reach her," Suor Rosa replied.

"Or maybe she just doesn't care."

They passed Susanna, lowering their voices.

"Then she shouldn't have said that Giuseppina could not be adopted."

Susanna waited until the nuns had rounded the corner at the end of the hallway, then hurried to the sickroom. On entering, she held her finger to her lips.

Pina was sleeping, her skin as pale as the cream-colored blanket.

Susanna shook her shoulder. "Pina!"

Pina slept on.

"Giuseppina!"

Pina opened her eyes, gummy with sleep.

"I overheard the nuns talking," Susanna whispered. "They sent a telegram to your mother. They told her how sick you are."

Pina sat up, throwing back the blanket. "They talked about my *mother*? But I don't have a mother."

"You must, after all. I heard them —"

"*Really?* You're not just pretending?"

"Really." Then Susanna hesitated. What if she'd misunderstood? Had it really been Pina the nuns were talking about? Yet she'd heard her name so clearly.

"Then Mammina must be coming here." Pina smiled. "Oh, Susanna! I never thought! The Virgin Mary saw my suffering. It was worth it after all. She's making my wish come true." Her cheeks flamed with color. "I will get better, starting this minute." Pina sat up straighter. "I will be healthy when Mammina comes."

"Well, it seems like your mother might *not* come," Susanna said slowly. "The nun said she didn't answer the telegram they sent."

"She didn't answer?" Pina asked in a small voice. She poked her finger into the moth hole in the wool blanket. "But I'm so sick. . . ."

"There was more." Again, Susanna hesitated, assuring herself that truly, it would be better to tell her everything. "They said that if your mother isn't ever going to come for you, she shouldn't have said that you couldn't be adopted."

"She said that?" Pina looked up at the ceiling. "Everything suddenly makes sense," she said after a moment. "Now I know why Suor Anna shook her head when that short woman smiled at me. It wasn't because I am naughty. It was because I'm not an orphan. I belong to someone. Someday my mother will come."

Susanna wondered if Pina's mother ever really would. Why hadn't she come in all these years? Maybe she was just trying to keep Pina for herself, even though she didn't really want her. "Yes," she forced herself to say. "That must be it."

Even her own father, who'd written a letter to claim her, hadn't come.

Pina went on: "Now I understand why *La Befana* brought me socks instead of a family. Even the angel knew. Everyone knew but me, it seems."

Susanna pulled at the edge of the blanket, straightening the wrinkles.

Pina laid her hand over Susanna's. "My *mamma* loves me. She wants me," she said. "Susanna! Do you know what this means? I have a mother!"

Pina's exuberance made Susanna inch away from her. Pina was getting too excited too fast. But she forced herself to say, "You have a mother the way I have a father."

"One father. One mother. We could be a family!" And Pina started laughing.

Susanna smiled for Pina's sake, but her mind whirled. Now Pina had a mother. But one who wouldn't come. And she herself had a father who didn't come. Whose parent would show up? Whose parent would take a daughter away? Would it be Pina abandoning her or the other way around?

Zeppole Di San Giuseppe

AT MASS ON PINA'S FIRST SUNDAY out of bed, she noticed the strangers who'd again gathered in the *chiesa,* looking over the girls as they stood on the wooden steps. Closest sat a man with a brown felt hat in his lap and a woman who nervously turned the pages of her missal.

But today Pina didn't care about these people. At last she didn't need them. She already had a mother. Mammina probably hadn't answered the nuns' telegram right away because she was busy. Maybe she was lending a hand to the Allies, helping Italy to recover from the war. When she was ready, she'd come.

During the time Pina had lain sick, she had imagined her mother. Because Pina had blond hair, Mammina had to be a northerner, unlike the dark people of the south, of places like Naples.

Instead of gazing hopefully at the strangers, trying to catch their eye, Pina looked at the white marble altar laid with the white lace cloth. She stared at the golden goblet polished to a mirrorlike shine.

As Padre Giovanni came up the aisle, swinging the censer of sweet incense, Pina lifted her voice and sang straight up to the ceiling, directing herself away from anyone who might want to take her from the *Istituto*. She already belonged.

"If you have a mother, why doesn't she come?" Elvira asked Pina as they waited in line for the bathroom after Mass.

Pina unbuttoned and buttoned her sweater. All the reasons she'd come up with for Mammina's absence suddenly seemed silly. "She's sick," she said at last.

The stall door opened. Carla came out, and Elvira went in.

"Your mother's been sick all these years?" asked Carla.

Pina stood on one leg and then the other. If only the line would hurry up! "Maybe she forgot where she left me."

Someone behind her in line snorted.

"My mother is an important person." Pina lifted her chin.

"Like Carla's?"

"Shut your mouth," said Carla.

"Probably she travels," said Pina. "Probably she works for the government or for the Allies. Or she sells jewelry to rich people."

"Hmm," said Donatella.

Finally, it was Pina's turn. After she'd closed herself into the stall, she wanted to stay there forever. With her sleeve, she wiped away tears. She heard whispers, running water, more whispers, then, "Pina! What's taking you so long?"

It was March and finally warm enough to go up to the tenth-floor *terrazzo*. Instead of playing bingo in the classroom that Sunday afternoon, the girls flew up the steps.

On the rooftop, everyone quickly organized into games. Lorena had brought up the jump rope. She and Bernadetta twirled it, while Donatella jumped, the rope slapping the tiles.

Others played Ping-Pong. The light ball

bounced—*click, click, click*—across the tiles of the *terrazzo*.

The air smelled of sweet wisteria, the flowers like soft bunches of purple grapes. Along with the corn husks, black uniforms and white sheets flapped from the clotheslines.

Pina gazed out at the tall buildings of Naples, the domes and carved pinnacles. She sat down in a chair by the big pots of lemon, tangerine, and fig trees, the figs with leaves like big hands.

Mammina had to be out there somewhere.

"Aren't you going to play Ping-Pong?" Susanna asked.

"I'm too tired from being sick."

"It's your saint's month." Instead of celebrating birthdays, the nuns celebrated the girls' saints' days. "You should be happy."

Pina was named after Saint Giuseppe, who was honored not just for one day like the other saints but throughout the whole month of March.

After March dinners, each girl got one *zeppole di San Giuseppe*. But because of her name, Pina got two of the sweet handmade doughnuts dusted with sugar.

"Yes, it's my saint's month. But how can I be happy when Mammina hasn't come for me?" Pina said.

"Maybe she doesn't know it's your saint's month. Maybe she wasn't the one who gave you the name Giuseppina," Susanna said.

Pina sat up a little. But then she noticed a fat slug on the leaves of a tomato plant and slumped again. "If Mammina doesn't come soon, I'll never be adopted," Pina said. "Parents want younger girls. I'm already eleven."

Susanna sighed. "At least we're still together."

Pina scooted her chair closer to Susanna. "I'll have to find Mammina myself," she said. Until she spoke the words, she hadn't dreamed of such a thing.

"How will you do that?"

The slug inched closer to a green tomato.

"Suor Anna has to have her address. Otherwise, she couldn't have sent the telegram."

"But . . . ?"

"We'll sneak into her office and find it."

The shadow of a tall building moved across the *terrazzo*.

"That sounds dangerous," said Susanna. "We could get caught."

"If we do get caught, *you* won't be punished. You're never in trouble."

"And should I start getting into trouble now? The corn husks turned out badly."

"Friends help each other. No matter what," said Pina, getting up. She leaned over the wall of the *terrazzo,* looking down to the street below. It was full of cars moving this way and that. Everyone was going someplace while she stayed here. She let her tears fall over the edge, a small part of her joining the greater world.

But crying wouldn't get her a mother. She turned to stand in front of Susanna, hands on her hips. "You *must* help me find my mother. You must. Otherwise you'll go off with your *papà* and I'll be stuck here by myself."

A Visitor

DURING THURSDAY DINNER OF *RISOTTO* AND white beans, Susanna looked up as the big door opened. There stood Suor Anna, looking small and crinkled, beside a tall man with very dark skin.

The whole room jingled with the sound of spoons being set down. Susanna swallowed her *risotto* without chewing: not only a man, but a *nero*! She sucked in her breath. Suddenly, she knew who he was.

The man wore a dark-blue sailor's uniform. Holding a sailor's cap in his hands, he looked at one row of girls after another.

Susanna raised her own brown eyes, ready to meet his.

Finally, Suor Anna pointed toward Susanna.

Susanna shivered as Suor Anna led the man closer. At last, he stood on the other side of her table.

"This is a happy day for you, my dear," announced Suor Anna. "This man says he's your *papà*."

Susanna stood up, knocking her bowl with her elbow. She stared at the man. Her destiny had arrived at last. Her very own *papà*. The man who'd created her. A great lump rose in her throat.

He stared back at her, turning his cap around and around in his hands.

Susanna wondered if he too felt that tightness in his throat.

The room was still, as though everyone were watching a film. The nuns had all stood, and Suor Vicenza fingered the beads of her rosary.

This man's dark face looked even darker against the white walls of the dining room. He was dark like Christmas chocolate. His hair was shaved close to his head, so she couldn't see if it looked like hers.

When he smiled at her, his lips trembled slightly.

Susanna stood up. She wiped her hands on a napkin. Her big moment had come. The moment she'd be lifted out of the sea of girls and claimed.

What was she expected to do? She'd imagined throwing herself at him. Instead, she wanted to cover her face with her hands. Of all the girls, was he really here to get *her*?

The sailor began to walk toward the end of the table.

After a moment, Susanna walked too. There were so many others here to adopt. Others who weren't *mulatte*. There was the beautiful Pina, for instance. . . .

Everyone scrambled out of the way. The *nero* scooted aside a bench with his knee. Susanna knocked against Elvira, who knocked against her bowl of soup, spilling it.

They'd meet at the end. And then what? Maybe lights would flash and the world would break into a burst of music. Or he'd look at her and shake his head, as if to say no, he'd made a mistake. . . .

At last they stood facing each other, and Susanna studied him—the thin arch of his brows over his brown eyes. The sturdy nose. His lips light, like his palms.

Was she looking at an older, manly reflection of herself?

Did she look like him? It was hard to know, since she'd hardly seen herself except by accident in a window.

Susanna felt his eyes flicker over her, head to toe. What did he think of what he saw? Was he trying to figure out if she was indeed his daughter? Or if she was good enough? Again, she wanted to hide.

"Buona sera," the man said with a heavy American accent.

"Buona sera," Susanna replied. Should she address this man as James Green? Signor Green? Or as Papà? She'd pictured throwing herself into his arms. But she couldn't do that. She just couldn't.

"I heard about you recently from an officer who knew your mother's friend," he said, his Italian slow and deliberate. He turned his cap around and around between his hands. "Your mother herself didn't tell me about you. I'm sorry it's taken me so long to find you."

"But today you're here," she said softly.

"But for only a short time. I have an assignment in North Africa." Again, his eyes traveled over her. "When it's over, I'll come back."

Susanna nodded. If he was coming back, he must be satisfied with her, for now at least. If he went away and came back, it'd give her time to get used to the idea of him.

Her *papà* held his sailor's hat with one hand and reached out—just a little—with his free hand.

In spite of herself, Susanna took a step back. She had never been touched by a man before. And never by anyone with skin so dark.

Her *papà* dropped his arm. He smiled, then bit his lip. *"Addio,"* he said at last.

"Addio," Susanna repeated. She wished she'd let him touch her. Now it was too late.

He turned and left, putting the cap on his head. He glanced back at her before slipping out, Suor Anna behind him.

The dining room erupted into a cacophony of voices.

"His uniform . . ."

"A real *papà* . . ."

"Susanna's so lucky."

"He's so tall."

But so dark, Susanna thought, in spite of all her wishes.

She left her dinner and hurried to the dormitory, where she drew the curtains back and examined herself in the window glass. Did she look like the man she'd just met? Was there any proof that she was his daughter? Or if not, would he want her anyway?

The quality of the reflection was too poor to show the exact color of her skin. But she saw that her eyes were round and pretty. Her face, wide at the cheekbones, narrow at the chin, was a nice heart shape. Was she beautiful after all?

Name and Address

REARRANGING THE BLANKET over her desk, Pina made sure the edges didn't touch the floor. The room was mostly silent as the girls worked. They'd graduated from crocheting black berets to crocheting white baby blankets. Suor Vicenza had explained that the nuns sold the blankets to companies in America, earning money for the *Istituto*.

Susanna sat beside Pina, humming a little tune.

Of course Susanna was happily humming. *Her* wish had come true, Pina thought. She yanked at her yarn with the crochet hook. She couldn't help but feel she might soon be abandoned. Her friend might leave at any moment, the way Fiorentina had.

The door opened, and Pina looked up to see Suor Rosa. At four o'clock sharp she always came to check the girls' work. As Sorella made her way between the desks, Pina overheard her comments:

"Your stitches are too loose." "What's this large hole? Any baby would be cold under your blanket. . . ."

When she came to Pina, she pointed, saying, "That row's crooked. Undo it and start over."

When Suor Rosa turned her back, Pina held up an index finger on either side of her head, creating two devil horns. "I need to get away from that old *diavola*," she whispered to Susanna. As she tore out the crooked stitches, she grumbled, "We never have time after school to play now. Every day the nuns keep us working all the way till dinnertime."

"They need the money."

"And they work us to death to get it." Pina leaned across the aisle. "I have to look for my mother. And you have to come with me."

Susanna shook her head. "If I get caught, my *papà* might not want me anymore."

Pina set down her crocheting and held up all ten fingers. "This is how long we've been together, Susanna. Ten years. For all that time, we've been like this." She crossed two fingers. "And now when I ask for something really important, you say no."

Susanna said nothing.

The crooked row torn out, Pina began to crochet again. She knew that this row would also be uneven, but how could she crochet with her whole life at stake? She let out a little hiccup of a sob.

"I suppose . . ." Susanna said, her voice so quiet that Pina had to choke back another sob to hear, "if you need me that badly . . ."

After eating dinner and preparing for bed, Pina and Susanna lumped up their blankets and pillows.

"Don't tell," Pina said to Donatella, who was watching with wide eyes. "We're not just fooling around."

"We're getting ready to find Pina's mother," Susanna added.

"Cross my heart," said Donatella. Then she touched her lips as though to seal them.

Pina and Susanna sneaked away to the *chiesa* to wait in the small, hot box of Padre Giovanni's confessional.

"Look what I got from the kitchen," said Pina, showing Susanna a candle and matches. "We'll need these so no one sees too much light."

The wooden walls of the confessional were carved with small designs that let in air so the person confessing could breathe but not be recognized.

Through these cutouts, Pina watched the *chiesa*.

It would never turn completely dark because of the bank of candles.

When the windows finally darkened, Pina swung open the squeaky door of the confessional. She beckoned Susanna, then led the way through the *chiesa*. Her shadow, cast by the soft candlelight, bloomed on the wall.

Pina paused at the entry to the hallway. She felt Susanna's breath on the back of her neck. Pina took one step out, then another.

When they arrived at Suor Anna's office, Pina put her hand on the doorknob and hesitated. If it were locked, all would be lost. She would never find her mother. But the knob turned easily, and Pina slipped inside with Susanna close behind. She shut the door.

In the darkness, Pina struck a match. It hissed as she held it to the candlewick. She waited as the circle of light spread, revealing Sorella's heavy wooden desk.

Susanna pulled open the drawers while Pina hovered with the candle. Pencils and pens lay neatly arranged in one. Paper in another. And finally, in the largest drawer, stacks of cardboard folders were lined up, labeled with names.

"Here, hold the candle," Pina said. She ruffled through the folders: Elvira, Antonetta, and Georgina together in one file, Donatella. "Here's mine," she said, tugging the folder out of the drawer. She spread it on the desk.

"Ouch," Susanna whispered as hot wax dripped on her hand.

Pina opened the folder. Inside were school report cards and medical records, including documentation of her recent sickness. And there, finally were the words: *Mother: Patrizia Esposito.* And an address. Clipped to this paper was the receipt from the telegram.

From another drawer, Pina took paper and a pen. Quickly, she wrote down the name and address. She tucked the precious information into her pocket.

Her breath trembled as she blew out the candle in Susanna's hand.

But how would they sneak out of the *Istituto*? Once they were back in bed, Pina turned her mind to this question. If they could just get out, she reasoned, all would be fine. She'd find her mother and wouldn't have to worry about the nuns ever again. Maybe if Susanna's sailor father never came back, she could live with Pina and her mother. Susanna could be her sister. . . .

Pina fell asleep imagining the dwelling that went with the address. It'd be a white marble *palazzo* with a courtyard of sweet white gardenias. She and Mammina would listen all day to the delicate sound of water falling from a fountain.

A Well-Behaved Girl

"SUOR ANNA, I HAVE SOMETHING to ask you," Susanna said, standing before Sorella's desk, her eyes pinned to the crack on the wall behind.

Sorella took off her reading glasses and laid them on the desk. "What is it, my dear?"

Susanna took a breath. "Pina and I would like to deliver some of the crocheted baby blankets to the nearby office."

Sorella toyed with her glasses, turning them in a slow circle on the desktop. "And why is that?"

Susanna rocked from one foot to the other. Sorella had asked her the very question she'd feared. "We make the blankets," she said as evenly as she could, "but we never see where they go afterward. It would feel more fulfilling if we could, ah . . . see the place."

The lie felt terrible. It was like the crooked crack that ruined the wall's smooth surface. But she was lying for Pina's sake, she told herself. Pina had to have a mother. Would Susanna's *papà* understand what she was doing for Pina?

The wrinkles of Sorella's white face deepened. She turned her gold ring.

Susanna heard a cart, perhaps of laundry, being wheeled down the hallway.

At last Sorella asked, "How did you feel on seeing your father?"

Susanna started. "My father?" What did Sorella mean? "Good. I felt good."

"Sit down, Susanna." Sorella paused until Susanna had positioned herself on the very edge of the narrow wooden chair. "Meeting your father may have felt good. But I'm sure your feelings were more complex than that."

Susanna scooted back, clasping her hands in her lap. Sorella really wanted to listen. "It seemed that I ought to have known him," Susanna said slowly, "but I didn't."

Sorella smiled. "It's natural that you'd have mixed feelings. You thought you were an orphan all these years, and now . . ."

"Yes," Susanna agreed. Then she leaned forward. "Sorella, do that man and I look alike?"

Sorella laughed. "Like father and daughter."

Susanna gazed down at her clasped hands, the square nails, the skin the color of *cappuccino,* saying slowly, "I wonder who my mother was. If she was Italian. What she was like."

Suor Anna examined her ring as if for the first time. "Perhaps one day you can ask your father these questions."

Susanna nodded. But her questions were so intimate. How could she ask them of a stranger?

Another cart passed down the hallway.

"You're a well-behaved girl, Susanna," Sorella said when the rumble of wheels had passed. "You're never in trouble. Your request to go out with Giuseppina is granted."

Red Pepper

"IF ALL GOES WELL TODAY," Pina said, "I'll find my mother. I'll never have to see this place again." She glanced back into the gloomy interior of the dull white staircase leading up and up.

She and Susanna both giggled, standing in the archway leading out to the street. Susanna held the bulky package of baby blankets under one arm. Pina took Susanna's hand, asking, "Which way shall we go?"

"To the right," Susanna replied.

"How do you know?"

"I just have a feeling."

The air smelled of spring flowers mixed with the fumes from vehicles. Pina pushed her way through the crowd on the sidewalk, clutching Susanna's hand, pulling her along.

They passed the building where they were supposed to deliver the blankets.

"Shouldn't we . . . ?" Susanna said, slowing down, taking the package from under her arm.

"On the way back," Pina insisted, moving forward, keeping her eyes down. "Don't look at anyone," she cautioned. The nuns always said that. There were things that could lead a person into sin. But now Pina worried that her face might betray her own sin.

Once they were a good distance away, with no sign of the tall, square mass of the *Istituto,* Pina laughed and lifted her gaze.

"Don't look up at temptation," Pina said, mimicking Suor Rosa.

"And she doesn't mean Monte Vesuvio," said Susanna.

"She means that statue of the naked cherub peeing into the fountain." Pina pointed.

"Since we don't know the way, why don't you ask that *carabiniere*?" Susanna gestured toward the officer in his red-and-black uniform, his narrow waist outlined with a leather belt.

Pina strode up to the policeman. "Signor," she said, "can you tell me where this address is?" She held out the piece of paper.

He glanced, then lifted his arm. "That way. It's a long walk." He moved off.

"If only he'd offered to go with us!" said Pina when the *carabiniere* was out of earshot. "It's so far!"

They passed shops selling salami hanging by hooks in the window and one selling only thimbles; another, frothy bridal gowns. They held their noses at the smelly fish market. They passed a *palazzo* with a courtyard full of fiery orange bougainvillea.

Pina felt sure they'd sung a funeral in that *palazzo*.

"Now which way?" asked Susanna as they came to a fork in the road.

A man was selling *gelato* from a small cart.

Pina held out the piece of paper, crinkled and damp from her sweaty hands.

The man waved it away. "I don't read."

Pina read the address aloud.

"That way." The man pointed left.

As they started down the left fork, Pina looked around. "We're close!" she breathed. "Maybe Mammina is somewhere here on the street."

"She might be that one with the red shopping bag," Susanna said, "or that one with the flowered hat, or that lady with the three children."

"If she sees me, she'll come running. She'll gather me into her arms. She'll squeeze me tight."

"'My *bambina*!' she'll cry," said Susanna.

Pina slowed. "But how could she know me? It's been a long time. She might not recognize me."

They passed a group of old women sitting in chairs on the sidewalk, a group of old men throwing down cards in a game of *scala quaranta*.

"Wait a moment." Pina undid her braids. Her hair fell like a soft cloud around her shoulders. She fluffed it with her fingertips, wishing there was a window to see herself in.

The name of Mammina's street was painted in fading letters on the side of a building. The sidewalk was littered with lemon and watermelon peels, scraps of old newspaper blowing in the warm breeze.

"Now for the number," said Pina.

As they walked down the street, which twisted up and down the side of a hill, Pina saw that the numbers weren't in order. Thirty-two was followed by ninety-four. There was no fifty-six. She wiped her forehead with the back of her hand. Maybe she'd copied the address wrong. Or maybe it didn't exist. Maybe the telegram had never arrived after all. She felt like crying, or like stamping her foot.

Susanna asked directions of a woman selling a wheelbarrow full of helmets left behind by various armies.

"Five buildings down." The woman pointed.

Finally, they arrived at fifty-six.

Number 1 was a bottom-floor apartment, a *basso*. Overhead, drying underwear in all sizes hung from the balconies.

This couldn't be it, Pina thought. Not this poor ground-floor place on this dirty street. It wasn't what she'd imagined. But the address matched.

Pina approached the carved wooden door. Pieces of the carving had broken off. She lifted the knocker. Should she let it fall? In a moment she might be face-to-face with her mother. Would she recognize this person? Would her mother recognize *her*? Would it be better to go on dreaming? Pina took a deep breath and let the knocker fall.

A man, a cigarette dangling from the corner of his mouth, his shirt untucked, answered the door.

"We're looking for Signora Esposito," Pina

said. Maybe, she thought suddenly, this man was her father!

"She's not here now."

Pina held up the paper bearing her mother's name. Had they come so far for nothing? Should she ask him if he had a daughter named Pina?

The man barely glanced at the paper. "She's not here," he repeated.

"Did she get a telegram?" Pina asked.

The man shrugged.

Pina's face fell. "Where is she?" she asked. She leaned against the doorjamb, her lip trembling. They'd come so far. Had Mammina moved away? Had she—the terrible thought arose—moved away *because* of the telegram?

The man threw his cigarette into the street. He shuffled from one foot to the other. "Gone shopping."

So she still lived here! "When will she be back?" Pina demanded.

Again, the man shrugged.

"Are you my father?" Pina asked.

"Your *what*?" He stared at her, then said, "Are you crazy?" He went back inside the apartment, shutting the door behind him.

Pina plunged her face into her hands and sobbed.

"We'll have to go back," said Susanna, putting an arm around her. "We can try again another day."

"But *how*?" Pina's plan to never return wouldn't work now. They'd both be caught. How would they ever get out again?

As they traced their way back, dusk fell. Several times Susanna had to ask the way.

Pina's feet hurt, and she was hungry. She almost longed for the comfort of the *Istituto*. Her heart was as heavy as a stone. "What if we're lost?" she asked Susanna. "What if we never find our way home?"

Susanna didn't answer.

As the shops closed, the *luminari,* the decorative lightbulbs strung over the streets, switched on. They illuminated a man lurking in the darkness between two buildings.

On seeing the man, Pina cried, "What if we get kidnapped? What if we get taken far away?" She'd longed to join the outside world. But not anymore.

Susanna took hold of Pina's arm.

When they got to the place to deliver the package, it too was shut.

"I know the way from here," said Susanna.

But they took a wrong turn and ended up at a park.

"The nuns brought us here once," said Pina.

"Not here," said Susanna. "That park had a fountain."

Pina looked around in the darkness. She'd lost all sense of direction. Where had the sun set? Where would it rise? Would they still be lost when it did rise?

"Look," said Susanna, pointing. "Over there— our building."

"Oh, yes!" Pina shouted. "That's our *terrazzo* on top."

As they walked away from the park, Pina kept the gigantic building in sight. When they finally arrived in front of the *Istituto,* she felt she could never climb those stairs. She couldn't face whatever awaited her at the door of the *Istituto.* She and Susanna had been gone far longer than necessary. And they hadn't even made the delivery.

She dragged herself up the seven flights she'd flown down earlier. Maybe, she dared hope, no one had missed them.

At the top, Pina stood on the landing and tried the big door. It was locked. She looked at Susanna.

"You'll have to knock," she said.

"But then they'll *know.*"

"They already do."

Pina knocked. Her fist felt small against the thick door.

Nothing happened.

She knocked again. Susanna joined her.

This time, the door was opened by Suor Rosa. She stared at them, her hands on her hips, her red veins blooming on her cheeks. "Where have you girls been?" she asked at last.

Pina swallowed hard. "Outside."

"Outside doing *what*?"

"We went to deliver the baby blankets." Pina now carried the package, holding it against her chest as a buffer.

Suor Rosa glanced at the package. "So you went to make a delivery, and what happened?" She grabbed the blankets and dropped the package with a thud.

"We—we—got lost. . . ." Pina stammered.

From behind her back, Sorella brought a piece of an old broken chair. "Hold out your hands, Giuseppina." She smacked Pina's palm three times.

Pina sank her teeth against her lip, biting back

tears. She'd only wanted Mammina! Sorella had no right!

When she finished, Pina tucked her hands in her pockets. Were they broken, like the old chair? She bit her lip harder.

"Hold out your hands, Susanna."

As Sorella prepared to strike, Pina grabbed Sorella's arm, shouting: "That's not fair! Susanna was just helping me!"

"Helping you do what?" Sorella's voice was as sharp as the knife that killed the Christmas chickens.

"We were trying to find my mother."

"What do you mean?" Sorella grabbed Pina's arms and shook her.

"I want Mammina!" Pina cried. She tasted blood.

Suor Rosa fished in her pocket and brought out a bottle. The label read RED PEPPER. "Open your mouth, Giuseppina," she commanded.

Pina clamped her mouth shut.

With her tough fingers, Sorella pried Pina's lips open. She thrust in the bottle and tapped hard.

"Oh!" Pina cried. Her mouth was on fire! She bit down on the bottle, on Sorella's fingertips.

She couldn't help but cry now! And cough! And choke!

"No more talking back, Giuseppina." Suor Rosa put the bottle in her pocket. "Your hair is a mess. Go braid it."

When Suor Rosa had marched off, the package of blankets under her arm, Pina slid to the floor, her back against the wall.

Susanna sat down beside her and put a hand on Pina's knee. "That old witch can't stop us. We'll try again."

A Sailor's Cap

IN LATIN CLASS, Maestra Artura had conjugated the verb "to love" on the blackboard. Maestra Adrianna pointed to the chalk-white words with a stick, while the girls recited: *Amo, amas, amat . . .*

Susanna stifled a yawn. Yet it felt good to be back in the classroom, doing ordinary things. She needed time to think quietly about her *papà*. She needed time to recover from the ordeal with Pina.

After the outing, Susanna had confessed her lies to Padre Giovanni in the tiny confessional. He'd assigned her five Hail Marys and three Rosaries.

Suor Rosa had banished Susanna and Pina from the dinner table for a week. Yet before bed each night, Suor Vicenza had eased their hunger, arriving in the dormitory with the sleeves of her habit filled with bread and slices of yellow American cheese.

Suor Anna's response had been the most difficult. Wrinkles etching her white face, Suor Anna had said simply, "I'm disappointed in you, Susanna."

Susanna had hung her head. Now, recalling Suor Anna's disappointment, shame rose in Susanna like a blush of red marinara sauce.

Just then, Suor Anna entered the classroom.

Maestra Adrianna paused, her stick frozen over *amamus.*

With a rustle of her black habit, Sorella walked quickly to Susanna's desk.

Susanna gripped the thick edges of her grammar book. Was Sorella bringing bad news? Had her *papà* been told about what she'd done with Pina? Did he not want a liar for a daughter?

Sorella bent down to whisper: "Your *papà* is here to see you."

Susanna closed her book, her hands trembling. He was back from North Africa! He'd kept his promise!

The recitation continued: *amatis, amant,* while Susanna followed Sorella into the *stanza della compagnia.* There the man sat straight and tall on the narrow sofa, this time in a white summer uniform. He stood when she came in.

She tried to recall what she'd seen of herself reflected in the glass. How did her looks compare with his? Her skin was much lighter. Her nose was narrower. They both had brown eyes, of course. They both had the same long, slender fingers. Beyond that, she couldn't tell.

Now that he'd stood to greet her, what should she do? Surely he didn't expect an embrace. But she should make some gesture of welcome. She offered her hand.

His grip was firm, his skin cool and dry. His long fingers met hers.

And then they both sat, Susanna on a chair opposite. She needed to make conversation. "How was Africa?"

He laughed. "Very hot."

"What did you do there?"

He laughed again. "I wish I could tell you, but my work is top secret."

She searched her mind for another question. The clock ticked the way her heart ticked with nerves.

Questions about her mother had been forming in Susanna's mind like summer thunderheads, filling the sky of her life.

But she didn't know this man well enough to ask these questions. She didn't even know if he really *was* her father and could answer them honestly.

"This place gives me the creeps," he said, looking up at a painting of Jesus. "I don't like seeing people's hearts floating outside the body."

Susanna studied the painting. She'd seen the image of Jesus's bleeding heart all her life. It seemed normal to her.

"How about if we get out of here?" he said. "Go someplace. Think they'd let you?"

"Only if *you* ask."

"Very well." He stood and crossed to the door, his shiny black shoes reflecting the room.

He'd left his white sailor's cap on the sofa. When Susanna heard his footsteps retreat, she reached out and picked up the cap. She turned it around in her hands the way he did. Then, without planning to, she lifted it quickly to her nose. It smelled of spicy hair oil and a muskiness she took to be a man's odor. It was an intimate smell. Smelling it, she'd gotten close to him, far closer than an embrace. She put the hat back on the sofa and folded her hands in her lap.

If this James Green got permission from the

nuns, she'd be alone with him all day. How could she spend so much time with a man? If he was her *papà,* that was different from being just *any* man. But what if he wasn't her *papà* after all?

The only other man Susanna knew was Padre Giovanni. She thought of his wavy brown hair and gray eyes, his ankle-length black robe. After Mass, he quickly left the *Istituto,* never staying for pizza lunch. He never spoke to the girls except from the other side of the confessional, from which, in exchange for sins, he doled out penances.

The man—Signor Green? Papà?—came back, swinging the door wide. He picked up the cap, and Susanna wondered if he sensed her secret touch. Had she put the cap back exactly as he'd left it? He gave her a big smile, his teeth white against his dark face. "All set, *bellissima.* Let's go."

He'd called her beautiful. And with a few words from him, one of the nuns had released her. Even during Latin class.

Susanna decided to think of this man as Papà, though she wouldn't say the word aloud.

As they walked down the seven flights of marble steps, their footsteps synchronized, Susanna thought that this time she wasn't sneaking out. She was going legitimately, with her father. Her father who'd called her beautiful.

Papà made his way through the crowd to the curb. He lifted his arm, and a yellow taxicab pulled up.

Papà held the back door open, then sat up front and directed the driver to take them to the port. Susanna had ridden only in the buses the school hired for trips.

She noticed that the driver looked out of the corner of his eye often at Papà. Was it because Papà was one of the Allies? Someone to be honored and respected?

Or was it because he was a *nero*? A curiosity. Perhaps not good enough to ride in the man's taxi. Maybe the man was having second thoughts about picking them up. Susanna noticed him studying her in the rearview mirror.

If she lived with Papà, they'd always be looked at this way by Italians. Her whole life she'd been teased by the girls of the *Istituto*. She wondered what it was like for *neri* in America. She'd heard there were many—surely people wouldn't stare. She and Papà wouldn't be such oddities for a taxi driver.

As the taxi idled in traffic, the driver honked often, placing the heel of his hand on the horn, pumping it in quick bursts. Once the taxi swerved, narrowly avoiding a man pulling a block of ice across the street.

This taxi ride reminded Susanna of the carnival where she and the other girls had driven tiny, bright cars. They'd bumped the cars into one another, laughing.

As the taxi rounded a corner, Susanna recognized an old building with the wrought-iron railings falling off the balconies. "We sang at a funeral there," she said. She saw the widow standing in the arched doorway.

"You did *what*?" Papà asked, turning around to look at her.

"Sang hymns for a dead person."

Papà shook his head. "Now that's something I never heard of."

"The nuns have clever ways of making money to feed us."

Papà's brown eyes rested on her face, as though studying her for the first time. "Singing at funerals is a clever idea. But it's a sad idea."

Susanna watched the ancient building until the taxi made another turn. Papà was right.

Finally, the yellow cab reached the port where buildings had been bombed at the war's end. The walls lay in piles of pastel-colored rubble: light yellow, green, and pink. The standing walls had holes blown in them. A large rat dashed from one ruin to the next.

When the taxi stopped, Papà handed the driver some bills and stepped out. He hurried to Susanna's door to offer his hand.

The port was loud with the calls of men loading big ships, the calls of men arriving on small fishing boats with nets full of fish, the cries of the seagulls, the honks of the ships.

Across the bay, Vesuvio rose into the bright blue sky.

"It looks so peaceful," said Papà. "It's hard to believe it ever erupted. Look over there." He pointed out into the water, in the direction of Mergellina. "That's my home."

Susanna looked to see a white ship in the distance, small like a toy.

"One day I'll take you on it," Papà said.

Susanna glanced at him. He was planning a future with her, a future together.

They went to the Maschio Angioino, the haunted castle. When the woman in the booth handed over the tickets, Susanna noticed she was careful not to touch Papà's hand. Was that usual for ticket sellers, or was it because Papà's hand was black on one side and bright pink on the palm side?

Usually, on school trips, the talk of the ghosts rumored to live inside the huge towers made Susanna shudder. But this time, the thought of the drifting white shapes gave her a secret thrill—she was safe at the side of her sailor *papà*. Her *papà* who, like a detective, had hunted her down. Walking close, she pretended she was holding his hand.

As they admired paintings of portraits and landscapes on the velvety red walls, Susanna wondered if he really thought she was beautiful. Had he said it as a joke? Would her *papà* prefer a daughter who was completely a *nera*? Was he really going to take her?

Was she ready to be taken? She wondered what she herself wanted from this *papà*, other than protection from ghosts. As an American, one day he would surely return to his country. Did she really want him to take her with him?

The sound of English tired her ears. The few words she knew—*Good morning. How are you?*—stiffened her jaw. And if American cheese and powdered milk was bad, the rest of the food might be worse.

Perhaps Papà would always live on a ship. After all, he was a sailor. If so, might she live on a ship with him? Susanna's only experience of being on the water had been at the Bosco dei Tre Mari, where the rented rowboat had sprung a leak and they'd all had to swim to shore.

Maybe Papà could live on his ship and she could keep living at the *Istituto.* He'd come for her, taking her out on little trips like this one. Maybe they'd go all the way to the slopes of Vesuvio.

Jumping Rope

PINA TURNED THE END OF THE rope while Susanna jumped. The other end was tied to the branch of a lemon tree. Pina counted out loud: *"Uno, due, tre ..."* but her mind was reliving the trip to Mammina's *basso*. Why was her mother in that awful place? Maybe she was only staying there temporarily. Pina felt sure that Mammina really lived in a *palazzo* with a cherub fountain. She'd imagined that *palazzo* in such detail—it had to be real!

If only Mammina would come to the *Istituto* to claim her. If only she'd treat her to an outing, the way Susanna's *papà* had. Even that would be something.

Pina stopped counting and dropped her arm slightly. The rope slackened, and Susanna cried out. "Sorry!" said Pina, lifting the rope once more in a high arc. "Thirty-three ..."

While Pina counted Susanna's jumps, she turned her mind to her mother again. The man might have told Mammina that her daughter had come. Maybe Mammina hadn't visited the *Istituto* because she expected Pina to go to her *basso*.

"Thirty-nine, forty . . ."

She had to look for Mammina again. She was willing to risk more of Suor Rosa's punishments. Her hands had been red only for a day and had hurt only for three days. And because of Suor Vicenza's kindness, she and Susanna hadn't gone hungry after all. It had been worth the pain to find Mammina's *basso*.

"Forty-six, forty-seven . . ."

Pina interrupted her counting again. Susanna had been jumping way too long. Pina had already counted to fifty-one. "We need to go look for my mother again."

"I—know. . . ." Susanna panted, still jumping.

"Maybe Suor Vicenza would come with us. That way no one could punish us."

Susanna tripped, and Pina dropped the rope.

"The sooner the better, Susanna. Your *papà* took you to the Maschio Angioino," said Pina. "Next it'll be America." She looked out over the rooftops, picturing the green Statue of Liberty holding out her freedom flame for Susanna.

"I may not go anywhere, Pina. I hardly know my *papà.*"

Jealousy burned Pina the way the rope burned her hand, but she forced herself to say, "Neither do we know the people who come here to adopt us. If this man is your *real* father, Susanna, you should be happy."

"Maybe he's not." Susanna bent to buckle her shoe.

"I don't know why you keep saying that. You two look alike."

Susanna picked up the rope. "That's just because we both have *nero* blood."

"It's more than that. The way you stand, leaning a little on one leg. The way you rub your foreheads with your fingertips." Pina demonstrated. "It's obvious."

"To you."

"You never look at yourself, so how could you know?" Pina stamped impatiently. She examined herself all the time in the window glass. She was more than ready to identify *her* parent. "Please turn the rope, Susanna. I'm ready."

The Aquarium

ON SATURDAY, Papà took Susanna to the aquarium, at the Mostra d'Oltremare. They stood close to the glass, gazing at the coral that looked like a plant but was really a colony of small animals.

Susanna thought of what Pina had said the day before. Did she and Papà really look alike? Did they share the same gestures?

This dimly lit room was a good place, Susanna thought, to ask the questions that nestled close to her soul, close to her very bones. Questions so raw that she might need to hide her face at the answers.

Gripping the ledge below the coral tank, she took a breath and ventured forth, "So my mother didn't tell you about me. She didn't tell you I existed."

Papà glanced at her, then stared back into the tank. "I didn't know her long."

Susanna studied Papà's profile. "Didn't you get along?"

"It wasn't that. The opportunity to see her didn't come up again. It was wartime."

Susanna had heard that Naples had been in chaos during the war. People lost track of one another. "What was her name?" she asked.

"Annabella." He beckoned her to the giant octopus. It swam lazily in the blue water lit from above.

"Annabella," Susanna repeated, letting the word make itself at home in her mouth. "What did she look like?"

"She had smooth, olive-colored skin and dark, curly hair. But"— he sighed —"I only saw her at night." A shark charged toward the glass of a nearby tank. "One night, to be exact." He lifted his eyes to the ceiling.

Susanna watched the knot of Papà's Adam's apple slide up his throat and back down again as he swallowed. She tried to absorb this news about her mother. Parents together for just one night didn't feel like a family. She looked at the stingrays fluttering through the blue water. "Do you know how she died?" she asked at last.

"In the bombing." Papà rocked back and forth on the heels of his shiny black shoes. "Right after your birth." He rocked more. "I learned that when I learned about you."

"Oh! How terrible!" Susanna exclaimed, stepping away from the stingray tank. "Did she die in one of the buildings near here? Why didn't she go into a tunnel?"

Papà shook his head. "I don't know the answers, Susanna. I wish I did."

Susanna leaned against the glass. The news made her whole body shivery.

Then, just as she'd imagined, Papà took her hand, enclosing her small one in his large one. "I'm sorry," he said. "You've had a rough beginning."

In silence, they watched a school of slim, golden fish.

"The nuns say I was laid on their steps by someone," Susanna said. "Do you know if that was my mother, or someone else?"

"I have no idea, Susanna. It seems you don't have much of an Italian family," he said, giving her hand a squeeze, then letting go. "Let's sit on the bench for a bit, and I'll tell you about your American family."

Her American family. Susanna had never imagined hearing those delicious words. "Please tell me everything," she said, seating herself beside him.

"I have one brother and one sister, both older," Papà began. "I'm the baby. We grew up in the city of Philadelphia, which is on the East Coast of the United States." The bluish light from the tanks blued Papà's dark skin.

Susanna listened carefully. Each of Papà's words felt like an anchor, securing her to her life.

"My father was a lawyer," he went on. "But the pressure of representing his clients in court killed him. He died young a of heart attack." He covered his face with one hand. "Dad was a good man."

Susanna inched closer. When Papà looked up again, she asked, "And your mother?"

"She spends all her time worrying about me." He laughed. "She wishes I'd come home. But enough sad talk. Do you like *gelato*?"

"Oh, yes!"

When they stood up, the light hit the fish tank perfectly, and she and Papà were reflected, side by side.

"There we are," said Papà.

"Do you —" she hesitated. "Do you think we look alike?"

He said something in English.

"What does that mean?" she asked.

"It means we look the same as two peas in the same seedpod."

Seeds in a seedpod. That sounded as though he was saying they were like members of the same family. The same.

They stood gazing, Susanna's eyes flitting from his face to hers, comparing.

"Don't worry," Papà said at last, putting an arm around her shoulders, pulling her in. "You're mine."

Their eyes met in the reflection, until Susanna smiled.

"Let's get that *gelato*," Papà said.

Susanna had visited the *gelato* stand in the company of the nuns and other girls. The vendor always gestured for Suor Anna to put her money away. Then he handed out free cups of *gelato* to everyone.

But this time Susanna didn't have to take the man's charity. Papà paid for her strawberry *gelato*.

As Susanna licked it, Papà's words—*You're mine*—echoing through her, she felt the sweetness of the whole world enter her.

Stigmata

MASS HAD JUST ENDED. PADRE GIOVANNI had slipped away through the side door, and Pina was ready to rush to the dining room for Sunday pizza.

But Suor Anna moved to the bottom of the steps and held up her hand. "Stay where you are, girls. I have an important announcement." She straightened the skirt of her habit and the beads of her rosary before saying, "Padre Pio has invited us for a special audience."

"Oh!" cried Pina.

Around her, other girls also cried out and murmured.

Whenever the newspaper published an article about Padre Pio, the nuns passed it around during religion class. On the streets, the magazines always had stories about the famous Franciscan monk. His picture hung in restaurants, his bright eyes staring out at the diners.

Padre Pio had the stigmata of Jesus. That meant he bled as if he really had nails pounded into his hands and feet. He even bled from near his heart.

All that bleeding sounded messy, Pina thought. And she didn't understand how Padre Pio's blood perfumed the air like fresh flowers. Whenever she cut herself, her own blood had a salty, earthy smell.

But Padre Pio performed miracles. It was that, and not the bleeding, that had gotten the girls excited. At the news of the invitation, Pina's heart danced against her ribs. Padre Pio understood that the girls of the *Istituto* needed miracles.

As everyone climbed down the wooden steps, Pina heard whispers:

"Padre Pio might find a home for both me and Antonetta," said Georgina.

"Or maybe my grandmother will bring more than chocolates," Elvira said, smoothing her red hair.

"My parents might decide not to be so busy," said Carla.

All day the school bus traveled through the mountains to Padre Pio's monastery in Foggia. Pina breathed deeply of the mountain air, wondering if this sweetness was Padre Pio's holy scent drifting their way.

As the bus rattled along the rough roads, Pina ran the glass beads of her rosary through her fingers. She begged the Virgin to tell Padre Pio ahead of time that she was looking for Mammina. If he knew her wish, how could he refuse?

She noticed Antonetta saying her rosary too. And Carla and Donatella.

"I've heard that Padre Pio can bilocate," Susanna whispered in Pina's ear. "He can be in two places at once."

"How can anyone do *that*?" Pina asked, dropping her rosary into her lap.

Susanna shrugged.

Pina wondered how it would *feel* to be in two places at once. Would all of a person be in the same place, or part here and part there? Bilocation would be a useful miracle next time she needed to look for Mammina.

At lunchtime, the bus stopped at a grassy field. The nuns passed baskets of sandwiches stuffed with fava beans and marinated eggplant.

By evening, the bus arrived at the stone

monastery in Foggia. As everyone filed into the church, Pina saw the Franciscan monks with their brown robes, the rope belts at their waists. "Look!" she said to Susanna, pointing at the monks' heads. Each had the very top shaved and a ring of hair around the bald spot.

Inside the church, Saint Francis looked down from a stained-glass window. The pews were full of people. Pina had thought it would be only the girls of the *Istituto di Gesù Bambino* here. It seemed that *everyone* was looking for miracles. Would Padre Pio use up his miracles before he got to her?

As Padre Pio said the Mass, Pina's rosary beads grew sweaty. Could Padre Pio *really* work miracles? Or was he as powerless as *La Befana*?

Padre Pio turned for his final blessing, the moment everyone had been waiting for. The people rose.

"*Dominus vobiscum,*" Padre Pio said.

"*Et cum spiritu tuo,*" the people in the pews answered.

"*Ite; Missa est.*"

"*Deo gratias,*" everyone replied.

Then Padre Pio faced the congregation.

Pina stood on tiptoe.

Padre Pio paused, then held up his hands. Blood trickled down the palms.

Pina gasped.

"Blessed Virgin," Antonetta whispered.

Pina glanced at Padre Pio's sandals. Did she see blood oozing from his feet, or was she only imagining things? And was that blood flowing from his side?

Padre Pio lowered his hands and left the church.

Everyone else began to leave too.

"Stay seated, girls," said Suor Anna. "Padre Pio will be back."

As they waited on the hard pews, Pina whispered to Susanna, "Did you see the *blood*?"

"Like tomato sauce."

"Shhh. Here he comes."

Padre Pio sat down in a big chair near the side chapel.

Everyone lined up and, one by one, Suor Anna pushed them between the shoulder blades. It was Antonetta's turn to kneel in front of Padre Pio. Pina rocked from one foot to the other. Was Antonetta asking for a mother for herself and Georgina? Would Padre Pio use up his miracles on Antonetta's wish? Would there be none left for anyone else?

This was worse than waiting in line for the bathroom!

When it was Pina's turn, she knelt like the others, her heart thudding like a captured bird. She gazed into his gray beard, breathing in the flowery smell of him. She stared at the cross-shaped scars on his hands. They weren't bleeding anymore. Pina wondered how he got the bleeding to stop. He must see that she had a special reason to be here, to request his miracles. He must take extra time with her.

But Padre Pio just lifted his hand and blessed her with the sign of the cross, and that was that. He beckoned to Susanna, and Pina stood up to make room for her.

Going home, they slept all night, rocked by the cradle-like movement of the bus. Tomorrow, maybe tomorrow, Pina repeated to herself, she'd know if Padre Pio was really a saint.

During school the next day, Pina waited to be called out of class. Would she be taken to the *stanza della compagnia*? Would Mammina be there for her, her eyes shining? Had Padre Pio summoned Mammina from her *basso*?

While the girls read aloud one by one about how the father of the beautiful Helen of Troy had been the god Zeus and how a war had been fought over her for ten long years, Pina watched the doorway. Surely a nun would come to say, *I must take Giuseppina.*

When it was Pina's turn to read, her tears dropped onto the page. Her voice choked.

"You must be tired from the trip, Giuseppina," said Maestra Artura. "Please read for her, Susanna."

Pina wiped her tears with her forearm. If Padre Pio wouldn't send Mammina, she would just have to go searching for her again.

Big Chickens

HIGH ABOVE, SUSANNA SAW AMERICAN SAILORS leaning over the railings of Papà's ship. Many were *neri* like Papà. But their skin wasn't all the same. Some were lighter, some darker, their faces the color of walnuts, of the bark of wet trees, of the rich soil in the potted trees on the *terrazzo*. They were as different-looking from one another as Italians. They looked nice in their white springtime uniforms.

Susanna followed Papà up the slope of the gangplank, over the deep green water that slapped back and forth between the dock and the ship. Today Papà was taking her on board to spend Easter Sunday.

Once on the deck, she looked out over the white-capped ocean and imagined traveling in this ship to America. It was certainly big enough— bigger than several *istituti* put together. And it didn't look as though it would sink in a storm like Robinson Crusoe's boat.

She noticed several Italian women. Girlfriends or wives of the sailors, she decided. Were they women like her mother, whom Papà had known for just one night?

Susanna looked back at the city, picking out the spires of the churches and the cathedral. The church bells rang to celebrate Jesus's rising from the tomb. Trees bloomed, their branches laden with lavender, white, and crimson.

Pina had cried bitterly at being left behind on Easter Day. As Susanna hugged her good-bye, she wished she could invite her along, but that was out of the question. It was miracle enough that Papà was taking *her* out. To invite a friend seemed impolite.

"We'll find your mother soon," she'd promised. "Very soon." She worried about what would happen to Pina if she left.

Papà led Susanna below deck, into the body of the ship. The motors hummed gently, making the floors vibrate.

When Susanna reached out to touch the gray metal wall, she felt the faint shudder of the big ship engines. The wall was cold against her fingertips.

She peeked into the little rooms they passed. All were gray. She'd thought the *Istituto* was dreary, but this ship was worse! How could Papà have brought her to celebrate Easter Day in such a place?

She grew conscious of the many men together in the belly of the ship. So many pressed close! So many voices speaking English! The unintelligible words formed a tangle of noise. She had an urge to run back up to the deck, where she could see out and listen to the church bells and the cries of the seagulls.

Soon the girls of the *Istituto* would walk in a line to the cathedral for Easter Mass. Susanna pictured the interior, dark and cool, smelling of sweet altar lilies. Joyful music would boom from the organ.

The hallway suddenly opened out into a large room. Although the metal walls were still painted gray, a bank of sweet white Easter lilies bloomed from a corner. Purple and yellow streamers hung near a platform where three sailors sat, preparing to play instruments. The long tables were set with white linen cloths and polished silver.

Papà pulled out a chair, and Susanna sat down across from one of the Italian women. The woman, whose earrings dangled and sparkled, smiled at her.

When everyone was seated, the tables filled, the sailors began to play. It wasn't church music or the music of the great composers that Suor Vicenza so loved, but rather jazzy, happy, American music.

Other sailors wearing aprons brought a big chicken to each table. They were the largest chickens Susanna had ever seen. They smelled of sage and rich juices.

Papà handed Susanna a bowl of dinner rolls. When she took one, it felt like a cloud. So white, so soft, it was like baby bread.

A bowl of something else white and soft came around.

"What is it?" Susanna asked.

Papà laughed. "Those are potatoes," he said. "They've been mashed with butter."

Susanna took a small spoonful.

The meat of the huge chicken was tough. "Why is the chicken so big?" Susanna asked.

Papà laughed again. "That's called a *turkey*. It's an American bird."

The woman across from Susanna winked, her earrings glittering.

After returning from the cathedral, the girls would eat the familiar Easter feast of braided bread filled with delicious *prosciutto,* salami, and hard-boiled eggs. All during Lent, when they'd eaten dried *baccalà* cooked in tomato sauce, they'd looked forward to the Easter feast. And now Susanna was here with this man, eating strange food.

The other sailors spoke to Papà in English, and he answered them in English.

Susanna listened hard for the few words she knew. How could she ever learn that awkward-sounding language? Italian flowed like a smooth stream, whereas the river of English bumped over rocks.

She suddenly felt very far from home. She longed for all that was familiar. She'd never dreamed she'd be homesick for the *Istituto.* She picked at the American food until her plate was clean.

Some of the sailors, who'd looked as if they enjoyed eating, stopped when there was still food on their plates. The ones who'd been serving carried off those plates.

Susanna stared. Was that food really going to be *thrown away*? Ever since the war, Italian people had been grateful for every bite. The nuns would never have allowed such waste!

When the table had been cleared, a sailor

brought a doll-size broom and dustpan. As the band launched into a new song, he swept the tablecloth clean of crumbs.

"Susanna," Papà said, reaching into his pocket. Was he going to pull out mints? *Biscotti?* That was what parents were supposed to do.

His hand was closed over something small, his dark fingers folded tightly. He opened his hand, and there on his palm lay a blue stone, like an Easter egg. It was attached to a fine silver chain.

"Oh!" said Susanna.

"This is for you." He held out the necklace. "So you won't forget me when I'm away."

Susanna had never seen anything so pretty. With thumb and forefinger, she plucked up the jewelry. The chain and smooth oval stone held the warmth of Papà's hand.

But she didn't know how the clasp worked and felt too shy to ask him to fasten it. She fingered the fine, slippery chain while nibbling at a dessert full of nuts and chewy dried fruit. Now that Papà had given her such a gift, she didn't feel homesick after all.

"Give me the necklace," Papà said softly.

Susanna started. She held out the fine silver chain, like liquid in her palm.

Papà lifted the chain and, leaning behind her, slipped it around her neck and fastened it. "That's better. Jewelry is to be worn, not hidden in a pocket."

As the necklace hung around her neck—the light chain, the heavier pendant—Susanna thought of how something of Papà had now been transferred to her. It rested right close to her heart.

After dinner, a sailor lowered a screen. Instead of a movie about the saints, an American cartoon flashed into life. Susanna laughed out loud at the bad, skinny rabbit, even though she didn't understand the words. She giggled at the funny sailor who punched people. She laughed to think of the sailors on this boat acting like that.

Papà laughed too. In order to see the screen, they moved closer to each other, their shoulders touching. Sometimes Papà translated for her, whispering a few words in his careful Italian.

Susanna felt as though she'd arrived on Robinson Crusoe's island after a shipwreck and a long time lost at sea.

After the cartoons, following Papà down the gray hallway, Susanna fumbled with the clasp of the necklace. Finally, it came undone. She slipped the jewelry into her pocket. It was safer that way.

Riding back to the *Istituto,* Papà sat in the back of the taxi with Susanna instead of up front with the driver. As the taxi drove under the arches of the *luminari,* he said, "I wish I could write you letters whenever I'm away. But I don't read or write Italian."

Susanna smiled. "At least you can *speak* Italian. You can *talk* to me."

"And in time you'll learn English," he said firmly.

Would she?

"Where's your necklace?" Papà suddenly asked.

"Here." Susanna patted her pocket.

"Why aren't you wearing it?" His voice roughened.

"I . . . I didn't want the nuns to see it. They might take it away." Papà didn't seem to understand that none of the girls at the *Istituto* had such luxuries.

"Take it away? They'd have no right to do that." He pounded one knee with his fist. "Those old witches," he muttered.

Susanna sat up taller. How could Papà call the

nuns witches? He mustn't! "The Sorelle have taken care of me all these years." Then words she'd pushed down burst forth. "You didn't come."

"I didn't know." Papà faced the window, so she saw only the back of his head.

"Why didn't you look sooner? Why did you leave me so long?" she insisted. She was on a downhill slide, unable to stop herself.

He turned his face to her. "I had no idea. None, Susanna." He shrugged, holding his shoulders high. His brown eyes were wide. "It wasn't until I ran into that officer that I learned about you."

Susanna stared straight ahead. The taxi wound in and out of traffic on the narrow streets. All the closeness of the cartoon watching had vanished. "If you'd been with my *mamma* longer, you could have taken care of her. And me. Instead of running off." The backs of her eyes prickled.

Papà sighed hugely. "If you're not going to wear the damn necklace, then give it back," he said.

She pulled the chain from her pocket, the stone dangling.

Papà held out his hand, the pink palm up. Then he pulled his hand back. "I'm sorry. Keep it. You don't have much else."

They rode the rest of the way in silence. Susanna felt shipwrecked all over again, lost at sea. Was this the end of being a daughter? Would Papà abandon her now?

She struggled to sort through her feelings, but they were as tangled as the noodles in a pot of spaghetti.

At the door of the *Istituto,* she offered her *papà* only a polite *grazie.*

Papà raised his hand as if to wave. But then he dropped his arm, saying quietly, "I'll be gone for a while."

"What's that?" Pina asked as Susanna slid the necklace into her *armadietto.*

"Nothing." She shut the little door.

"Let me see it. Please."

"It's really nothing."

"It's jewelry. I saw it. Your *papà* gave it to you, didn't he?"

Slowly, Susanna opened the *armadietto* and brought out the blue stone dangling from the chain. She held it close so the other girls wouldn't catch sight of it.

"Oooh," said Pina. "Can I try it on?"

Susanna thought of the quarrel in the taxi. "Papà wouldn't want you to."

"He doesn't have to know. You have a *papà* and I have no one, yet you won't let me wear that necklace just for a minute?"

"Just for a minute, then."

Pina turned and lifted up her blond braids while Susanna fastened the clasp. She patted the blue stone, declaring, "This means he's going to take you away. Any day." She made her way to the window and pulled back the curtain.

"Don't let anyone see. Here comes Antonetta!"

"It's so pretty," Pina said, turning back. "He must already love you."

He hadn't acted like it, though, Susanna thought. Not in the taxi. And now she was doing something that might anger him even further. "Please give it back now, Pina," she said.

My Darling Daughter

"YOU MUST COME WITH US, or Susanna and I will go alone and be punished again!" Pina said to Suor Vicenza.

"But it might not be proper for me to go." Sorella straightened the large white collar of her habit. "Suor Anna might say no."

"Tell her you *have* to come. You have to," Pina pleaded. "I'm looking for my *mother*!"

"But I'm only a *postulante.* I'm not even a real nun."

"But you can keep us safe, can't you?"

With the toe of her shiny black shoe, Sorella traced the outline of a white floor tile. "The situation with your mother upsets me, Pina. I don't like the way she keeps you here. Yet she never comes."

"That's right!" said Pina. "You understand!"

Sorella kept outlining the tile, this time with the other shoe. "It's a shame that years have passed with no solution. . . ."

"Will you go with us, then?" asked Pina, her palms pressed together as if in prayer.

"I'll tell you what," Sorella laid a cool hand on Pina's forearm. "I'll go, but I won't tell Suor Anna that we're doing such an important thing. I'll just say it's a small outing for fun."

So on Saturday, Pina, along with Susanna, both wearing their black-and-white-checked summer uniforms and their broad-brimmed hats, set forth, along with Suor Vicenza—her black robes flapping in the breeze.

Pina led the way. This time, she didn't need to ask directions but moved confidently down the sidewalk crowded with vendors selling pyramids of bright purple eggplant, tangerines, and pear-shaped tomatoes. She moved past the pizzerias and the smelly fish market. She led the others past the tiny thimble shop.

Today she had to succeed. The necklace Susanna's *papà* had given her was a sign.

She felt balanced, as though on the blade of a

knife, between excitement—Mammina might be home this time—and fear—she might not be. If she were, Pina was soon to be flooded with kisses and cries. And Susanna and Suor Vicenza, her two favorite people, would be her witnesses.

"This may be your happy day, Pina," said Suor Vicenza, breathing a little hard.

"I hope so! I hope so!" Pina sang out.

"I hope so! I hope so!" Susanna echoed.

They walked up Mammina's narrow street, Pina's nostrils full of the dusty smell of the stones. The morning had grown hot, and Pina moved impatiently around a pair of long-horned oxen, giving one a little shove as she passed.

When at last they came to the *basso,* Suor Vicenza gazed up to the balconies of drying underwear. She gazed as though she expected the apartment to be located above. The higher up, the more expensive the apartments. The street-level *bassi* were for the poor.

Pina wished she hadn't noticed Sorella's glance.

Sorella stepped forward, toward Mammina's door. "Let me speak to the woman."

But Pina ran ahead and lifted the knocker. No one needed to introduce her!

This time, the door was opened not by the man with the cigarette but by a blond woman. She blinked at the bright sunlight.

Blond hair! Pina touched her own. It was the same color! This was proof! Her heart danced.

"Mammina!" Pina cried. "Here I am! I'm your daughter, Pina. I'm Giuseppina." She threw her arms around the woman. She hugged her tightly.

And then she waited. Pina didn't feel any arms lifting for the embrace. The woman's body remained stiff and unresponsive.

Pina drew back. Had she made a horrible mistake? "Aren't you Patrizia Esposito?" she demanded.

The woman's eyes narrowed. "I am," she said, her voice husky.

"Then you're my mother!" Surely now the big moment, the moment of her dreams, would bloom like a scene on a giant movie screen. "Oh, my darling daughter!" Mammina would cry. Pina raised her arms again.

Patrizia Esposito just opened the door wider, stood back, and motioned the three of them inside. As Suor Vicenza passed her, she nodded slightly.

Pina looked around quickly at this *basso* that might soon—very soon!—become her new home.

Tatty green curtains clashed with the pink walls. The sofa in the corner was covered by torn lace. By the window sat a small round table with a clutter of dirty cups and saucers. A door led into another, darker room.

The woman gestured toward the sofa. "Please sit down."

Pina positioned herself and smoothed her uniform skirt, ready for Mammina to join her. Now that they were inside, out of the public eye, surely she'd put her arm around Pina's shoulder, squeezing her close, kissing her cheek. There'd be tears all around.

But instead Mammina chose a chair across from the sofa, over by the round table.

Suor Vicenza and Susanna sat down close to Pina, the sofa dipping on either side of her. This was all wrong! It shouldn't be *them* sitting with her. There had to be a misunderstanding! Pina gripped her skirt in both fists.

"I live at the *Istituto di Gesù Bambino,*" she said. "Where you left me. When I was sick, the nuns sent a telegram. Didn't you get it?"

Mammina gave a tiny nod.

Pina loosened the grip on her skirt. A dark feeling welled within her. "But you didn't answer?"

Mammina shook her head. "The nuns can take care of you better than I can," she replied.

"But I was so sick! I could have died!"

"The nuns have better medicine than I do."

How could Mammina be saying these things? How could she be so cold? Pina's lower lip began to tremble, and then tears—huge round ones—cascaded down her cheeks.

Suor Vicenza took Pina's hand.

Susanna slipped her arm around her shoulder.

Mammina sat unmoved by the window, her squarish jaw set. Was this the very mother that Pina had longed for? She wasn't nearly as cheerful and happy as the women who came to the *Istituto* in search of daughters.

"Why did you put me in the *Istituto*?" Pina cried out at last.

The woman—Pina couldn't think of her now as Mammina or even as Mother—leaned her chin in her hand. With her other hand, she twisted an empty coffee cup back and forth. "I was too young to keep you. I was only sixteen when you were born. The war was raging, and all was in chaos. There was hardly any food."

Pina felt Susanna's arm tighten across her shoulder. Sorella cleared her throat.

"But now you're older. . . ." Pina said. Surely, there was a way. . . .

The woman shook her head. "I still don't have the money to take care of you."

Sorella squeezed Pina's hand.

"I don't cost much," Pina protested. "I could sleep on the floor. I know how to crochet baby blankets. . . . We could sell what I make. . . ."

The woman didn't lift her face. "I have a new life now," she said quietly.

The room fell into silence.

Susanna sniffled.

Pina began to sob so hard, she coughed. She felt as though she'd hack her heart right out of her chest. Her heart would lie naked before Mammina, pulsing like Jesus's heart of suffering.

Pina peeked up to see that Mammina now sat with her face buried in her hands. Were her shoulders shaking—just a little?

A baby wailed from the room next door, a waking-up wail.

Pina sat up. "You've got a *baby*!" she said, wiping her face with the backs of her hands. "I could take care of it for you. I could learn how."

The woman lifted her face. Her eyes were red. Without looking at Pina, she got up and entered the small, dark room. The baby stopped wailing, but the woman didn't return.

That baby, Pina reflected, was like the baby *she'd* once been. Would Mammina give it up to a place like the *Istituto*? Or—Pina's heart pinched tight—would she keep that baby and love it as she'd never loved her?

As they waited, the clock ticked. The ticks were jerky and irregular.

Suor Vicenza took her rosary in both hands, her lips moving silently, the beads clattering softly in her lap.

Susanna brought out a rosary from her pocket.

Pina put her hand in her own pocket. But she didn't pull out the rosary. Instead she clutched the beads hard in her fist.

At last Sorella said, "We may get caught if we stay longer."

Pina pretended not to hear Sorella. In the other room Mammina was singing that baby a lullaby.

But she sang it too loudly, her voice rough and scratchy. She sang as though to drown out whatever was happening in the other room.

"We should go," said Suor Vicenza, rising from the bed. "I was foolish to have brought you here."

Susanna got up, but Pina remained. She couldn't give up so easily.

"Come, Pina." Sorella offered her hand.

Pina stared at Sorella's soft white palm, the extended fingers. At least *someone* wanted her. She put out her own hand and let Sorella lead her across the room.

Susanna opened the door to the bright afternoon and dirty sidewalk.

"I'm so sorry, Pina," said Suor Vicenza. "So very sorry."

Pina heard Sorella's words as though from a great distance. Was Sorella speaking to *her*? She looked down at a discarded banana peel. It had been stepped on many times. She gripped Sorella's hand tighter. She herself felt just like that bit of trash.

Come to Me

SUSANNA HAD BEEN SITTING in the *stanza della compagnia* for over an hour. She was dressed in a clean black-and-white-checked summer uniform, her straw hat neatly on her lap, waiting for her *papà*. The ceiling fan turned overhead, stirring the warm air. Outside, the hot *sirocco* was blowing.

Suor Anna had said he'd come at ten-thirty. The round white clock now read *eleven*-thirty.

There was so much traffic in Naples. Susanna recalled how slowly the taxi moved. Maybe Papà hadn't left early enough. Or maybe he'd had last-minute work to do on his ship.

The large hand of the clock was now edging toward the eight. Heat filled the room. There was no room for anything but the thick, suffocating air. No room for a tall *papà*. Susanna picked up a small prayer book and fanned herself.

It was too late. Papà wouldn't come. Maybe, remembering that fight in the taxi, he'd decided he didn't want her after all.

The blue pendant hung around Susanna's neck, underneath her blouse. That morning she'd put it back on. Even though the nuns might spot the thin silver chain, Papà should see her wearing it. Susanna placed her fingertips on the oval stone and pressed it, moving Papà's gift closer to her heart.

When the clock read eleven-forty-five, Suor Anna entered the room, shutting the door behind her. "I'm sorry, Susanna. You'd better come have lunch with us."

Susanna lifted her chin. She wouldn't cry. She didn't need a *papà* who lived on an American ship and ate strange American food. She'd rather stay here with the nuns.

Papà didn't come all that day, nor did he send word.

"Sorrento will cheer you up," said Elvira.

But as much as Susanna loved the beach, she was reluctant to leave the *Istituto*. "What if my *papà* comes looking for me and I'm not here?"

"It'd serve him right." Elvira tossed her red hair. "Besides, everyone's going, and you can't stay back."

"Besides," said Donatella, "it's too hot to stay in Naples."

Susanna took off Papà's necklace again and laid it in the drawer, underneath a pile of black winter socks.

The following morning, Susanna sat in the back of the big old green-and-white bus. She shared the seat with Pina, whose eyes had been puffy ever since the visit to her mother.

"Your father probably forgot to come," said Pina, opening the window.

"Or maybe he doesn't want me." Susanna closed her eyes.

"The way my mother doesn't want me," Pina said with finality.

Susanna took Pina's hand, lacing her dusky fingers through Pina's soft white ones.

During the long ride to Sorrento, the girls in the front sang Schubert's *Ave Maria,* their voices floating out the windows into the warm air. The bus passed fields of bright poppies, the happy red faces nodding in the breeze.

If she hadn't taken the necklace off that night, Susanna thought, if she hadn't spoken so harshly, so foolishly to Papà, she too might be singing the *Ave Maria*.

Papà must have thought long and hard about their last evening together.

And yet, it was cruel of Papà to just not come. Fathers were supposed to forgive their daughters, not abandon them. She thought of his talk of his American family. *Her* American family, he'd implied. And then he hadn't come.

When the bus stopped, everyone climbed out.

Beyond the sandy cliffs, Susanna glimpsed the turquoise ocean. Usually, her heart thrilled at the sight, but today it felt as dull and heavy as a fisherman's lead weight.

Pina woke up, rubbing her eyes. "Are we here?"

"Yes. Look."

The other girls already stood gazing at the water spreading toward the horizon like a length of silk.

"Let's get out," said Susanna, standing up.

Pina sighed, but she moved.

Outside the bus, Susanna breathed in the warm salty air. She wanted to fill herself with something other than longing. She loved coming to Sorrento, just loved it. She wouldn't let that man—that man who hadn't come, hadn't sent word—spoil the trip for her. She wouldn't.

Suor Vicenza led the way down the path, the black skirt of her habit tucked up.

On the sand, in wooden cabanas, everyone changed. As soon as Susanna put on the shorts and long shirt that reached her knees, she was glad she'd left the necklace at the *Istituto*. It could have gotten lost here in the piles of clothing, shoes, and straw hats.

But why would she want to keep it now? If her *papà* had abandoned her, she didn't need to think of him anymore. She could give the necklace to the nuns to sell for food.

The nuns emerged from their cabanas wearing black swimming dresses. They'd taken off the big white nun headdresses and wore only kerchiefs tied under their chins.

While the rest of the girls raced to the warm water, plunging into the tumble of waves, Susanna and Pina sat down near the tide line. Susanna scraped at the damp sand with her fingernails. Never would she trust that man again. Never. If he ever came to the *Istituto* again, she'd refuse to see him, even if she *had* said mean, foolish things.

Under the illuminating sunshine, Susanna wondered if perhaps Papà's absence had had nothing to do with the quarrel. Perhaps he'd decided he didn't want a daughter after all.

She dug up a clamshell, and Pina a black mussel.

The sun burned like a hot jewel. She'd be sorry later if she didn't swim. "I'm going in," Susanna announced.

Pina shrugged. "Go ahead. I don't feel like it."

The waves landed hard against Susanna's body. She almost enjoyed battling her way through them—the heavy water presented her with something real to struggle against. At last she got beyond to an area of smooth blue swells and lay on her back, letting the ocean rock her.

For a time, she languished in the hot sun. The warmth felt good with the cool water underneath her. For whole minutes at a time, she forgot about Papà. But when she heard the nuns calling from the shore, she roused herself and found her pain even sharper.

The nuns served lunch in the shade of the cabanas. As Susanna ate her sandwich of mortadella, eggplant, and long red tomatoes with olive oil, she thought of how lucky she'd been. She relived every moment of the visit to the haunted castle, to the aquarium, Easter Day on Papà's ship. She recalled the tender way he'd fastened her necklace.

"Lie in the sun on your stomachs," Suor Anna ordered when they'd finished eating. "If you get enough sun, you won't be sick in the winter."

As Susanna lay facedown, the sun pounding against her back, her tears seeped into the sand. Papà was gone now, and she felt utterly helpless. If he never came back, what would she do?

An idea began to form. It formed the way a grain of sand irritates an oyster until it builds a pearl. The pearl was her idea. She didn't have to remain helpless. She could send Papà a telegram. It was simple. She knew the name of his ship.

But telegrams were expensive and allowed few words. He'd sent the nuns a letter. Surely there was a place where she could send one back.

But Papà didn't read Italian. He'd told her that very clearly. She'd have to write in English.

Susanna sat up and wiped her tears with the back of her hand. She looked out at the sea, which now looked fresh and alive, full of promise.

That evening, with Suor Vicenza's help and a dictionary, Susanna sat down to write.

"How should I address him?" she asked Sorella. "As Signor Green, or as Father, or as Papà?"

"As Papà," said Sorella gently.

On pale blue airmail paper, Susanna wrote:

Esteemed Papà,

Come to me. I sorry. Please to come. You write english, I read.

I loving you.

Susanna, daughter of yours

She sealed the letter in a pale blue envelope.

Another *Basso* Visit

PINA LAY AWAKE in her dark bunk, the sounds of the other girls' soft breathing around her. She longed to rush out of the *Istituto* and along the streets she now knew so well. She'd knock on the *basso* door, and when Mammina answered, she'd throw herself into her arms again. This time she wouldn't let go. She'd hang on until Mammina softened and relented.

Every little bit of Pina ached for that embrace, but now the darkness opened, then closed back around her as Pina remembered Mammina's hard face, the way she'd sat far away across the room. The way she'd gone into the baby room and hadn't come back, not even to say good-bye.

Ever since that day, Pina had found little presents tucked under her pillow: a chocolate, a picture of the Baby Jesus, a tiny note—*God loves you.* These gifts of Suor Vicenza's, kind as they were, were crumbs when Pina was hungry for a whole cake. Suor Vicenza could never replace Mammina.

Pina tossed back and forth in the bunk. She beat against the truth that Mammina didn't want her as though pounding her fists against a locked door.

An old moon rose, barely visible through the curtains. When it had risen halfway up the window, Pina leaned out of her bunk. "Hey, Susanna. I'm going back there," she whispered. "I'm going to Mammina."

"Mmm?"

"I'm going to make Mammina see that I'm her daughter. I belong with her, not here."

Susanna yawned. "It won't work, Pina." She yawned again. "That Patrizia Esposito was very set against you."

"She doesn't know me."

"She doesn't *want* to know you."

The darkness closed in again. Pina tossed. "My *mammina does* want me," she said loudly.

"She won't let you go to anyone else, you mean."

Pina felt like covering her ears against Susanna's words.

"Maybe when you were a baby, she thought she'd come get you someday. But not now. Suor Vicenza says it's shameful the way she acts."

The blood rushed into Pina's head.

"You're the prettiest girl here, Pina. If Suor Anna would stop warning people away from you, surely someone would adopt you."

"Quiet!" someone said.

Pina lay thinking more. At first her mind twisted against Susanna's words. Somehow she *would* make Mammina own her. She would force that. But as Pina grew drowsy, her will softened.

Susanna's words eased into her, gently asserting their truth. By morning, the words rang in Pina as clearly as the church bells that tolled throughout the city.

During class that day, when Pina heard the sound of the bread delivery truck pull up outside, the brakes crying loudly, she pretended she had to go to the bathroom. As the delivery man propped open the door and carried in the big bags of loaves, Pina slipped out.

Her mission was worth any punishment.

She hurried down the streets, crying, *"Scusami!*

Scusami!" Her heart pounded. Soon Maestra Artura and Maestra Adrianna would realize she hadn't returned to class. They'd tell the nuns. Suor Vicenza would know where she'd gone and would have to tell.

Running, Pina looked back over her shoulder, searching the street for a black-and-white nun's habit. She mustn't be caught now. Once, she knocked into a donkey hauling a load of firewood and scratched her arm.

As she ran, a thunderstorm started to build, the clouds massing above the rooftops.

In front of the *basso,* Pina paused, catching her breath, her uniform damp with sweat. No one could stop her now. But did she really want to cut herself off forever from her mother? Did she want to make that demand? Glancing around, she recalled the certainty of the early morning. She had to hurry.

When Pina knocked, Mammina called out, "Who is it?"

"It's me, Pina. Giuseppina."

There was a long silence before Mammina spoke the words, "Come in."

She was sitting at the round table with the

baby. Pina couldn't tell if the baby was a boy or a girl. She only wished it wasn't there.

Pina sat down on the sofa. The lacy spread lay in a heap on the floor.

"What do you want this time?" Mammina said.

Pina took a deep breath and spoke the words she'd rehearsed in her head. "I know you don't want to be my mother. It's time for you to let someone else have me."

The baby stood up on Mammina's lap, beginning to fuss. It grabbed Mammina's blond hair. It pulled her earrings.

Untangling the little fingers, Mammina said, "I know you're safe with the nuns. I don't want you living with anyone I don't know."

"But I don't *want* to stay with the nuns!" Pina almost shouted. If this woman had lived with nuns for so many long years, she wouldn't say such a thing. "I want a real family."

The baby fussed louder. Mammina jiggled it.

Pina suddenly hated this baby. It was now fretting so loudly that she and Mammina could hardly hear each other.

"I was so young back then," Mammina said, holding one of the baby's tiny hands. "I suppose I

was jealous at the idea of anyone else having you."
She glanced at Pina.

Jealous. Pina liked the sound of that. But
Mammina was no longer jealous. She had this
awful baby. Mammina didn't need an eleven-year-
old girl called Pina.

A hot wind blew the green curtains. Pina could
hardly look at that baby. She felt like plugging her
ears against its cries.

Outside, thunder rolled across the sky.

Pina wished that she too could fuss like that
baby. She longed to lean her head on Mammina's
shoulder to cry and cry.

Lightning blazed beyond the green curtains
and thunder again pounded the sky.

"I can write a letter to the nuns," Mammina
finally said in the break between thunderclaps.
"I'll tell them I've changed my mind on adoption."

"Really? You will really do that?" Pina almost
leaped across the room to hug Mammina. But then
she sank back, both elbows on the sofa. Convincing
Mammina had been so easy. Too easy.

"It's the right thing to do," Mammina said
firmly. She stood up, tucking the baby under one
arm. She rummaged in a drawer.

"I'll help you," Pina offered, getting up.

In the drawer the only paper was a receipt for bread. It would have to do. At the back of the drawer, Pina found a pen.

Now that it was time for Mammina to write the letter, the baby fussed harder. Mammina tried to get the baby to drink milk, but it pushed the bottle away.

"Here, hold her," Mammina said, shoving the infant into Pina's arms.

While Pina held the baby—*my sister,* she thought—Mammina wrote the note, penning the words that would free Pina.

At the end, Mammina took the baby and handed Pina the bread receipt with the note written in uneven block letters. "Good luck. I hope you make someone a good daughter." She bit her lip and grazed Pina's cheek with the back of her hand.

Outside, the church bells struck the hour.

"Quick. Get out of here. My husband will be home soon."

"He doesn't know about me?"

"Of course not. How could I tell him about your father? Go quickly."

Pina hurried across the room. She opened the

door, and with one last glance at Mammina and her baby, closed it behind her.

When Pina looked around for the nuns, instead she saw, making his way through the crowd, the same man who'd opened the door on the first day.

She hurried off in the opposite direction, clutching her straw hat to her head with one hand, the note with the other. One piece of paper had brought her to this place. Now another was taking her away from it.

The clouds had unfurled themselves across the sky. Lightning flared and the storm broke, drenching Pina.

By the time Pina reached the *Istituto,* the storm had passed. The clouds broke apart to reveal a clean, sunny sky. Pina paused to shake the water from her straw hat. She lifted her face to the sun, letting the warmth dry it.

She did indeed feel freer. Susanna had been right. She'd guided Pina toward being adopted. Susanna, instead of trying to hold on to her as Mammina had done, had helped Pina to free herself. She had Susanna to thank.

Bellissima

"CAREFUL!" SUSANNA CALLED TO PINA as she chased the Ping-Pong ball toward the fig trees. Clusters of bees swarmed around the ripening fruit.

She watched as Pina picked up the ball, avoiding the bees. But then Pina didn't return to the table but stood staring at something behind Susanna. She dropped the ball, and it bounced back toward the fig trees.

"What is it?" Susanna asked, then turned herself to see Suor Anna in her black habit and, behind her, Papà in his white uniform.

Susanna laid down her paddle. She reached to pull her socks straight.

Suor Anna led the way to two chairs near the pots of tomatoes. "It's a lovely evening." She gestured with her wrinkled hand. "Why don't the two of you sit here?"

She disappeared, her black skirt briefly catching on the thorn of a lemon tree, but neither Susanna nor Papà sat down. Susanna noticed her pale blue envelope in Papà's hand.

"I'm so sorry," he said, pinning her eyes with his. "I'm sorry I didn't come the other day. The nun told me you waited a long time."

Biting the inside of her cheek, Susanna looked down at the red tiles of the *terrazzo*.

"The Navy sent me on a secret mission," Papà continued. "I couldn't tell anyone."

She glanced up, meeting his eyes. Going on a secret mission sounded better than refusing, or forgetting, to come. "You couldn't tell even me?"

"Not even you."

She stepped forward. "You didn't go away because of the necklace?"

He frowned. "The necklace?"

"Because I took it off."

He laughed. "Oh, that. I'd forgotten."

Susanna smiled a little. Had her supposings been wrong? It seemed she'd *invented* all those hurtful stories about Papà.

"The nun told me you were upset when I didn't show up," he went on.

She bit her cheek again. Hard. But in the end she had to turn away. She felt like Vesuvio erupting, spewing forth all that had been held down, deep down, for so long.

"Oh, Susanna, *bellissima*. I didn't know you cared." Papà faced her around, pulling her into an embrace.

She cried into the starched white of his sleeve. Though she shook with sobs, he held her without wavering. After a while, the intervals between sobs became longer, until Susanna coughed and grew quiet.

He held her at arm's length and put his sailor's cap on her head. It fell down over her eyes, and she laughed, tipping it back up.

"Papà," Susanna said. The two syllables rolled into the air.

"*Figlia?*" he responded, lifting his eyebrows questioningly.

"Yes, *figlia*." Yes, she was his daughter.

"Let's sit down," Papà said. "I have something to show you."

Susanna scooted her chair close to Papà's.

He took out his wallet and eased something from it. "This is your family," he said, holding a stack of what looked like photographs.

Her family. Again, Susanna experienced those delicious words.

"Here's your grandmother," he said, handing over the first picture.

Susanna saw a woman with wiry hair like her own, her knotty curls tinged with gray. The woman had a nice, wide smile.

"And this is your grandfather, who's dead."

Susanna took the photograph carefully by one edge. The man wore a black suit and had his arm around a small boy.

"Who's that?" Susanna asked. "He's cute."

"That's me." Papà flipped quickly to the next picture. "And here's your auntie and uncle," he said. "And look—this is your cousin, Deborah. She looks like you."

Susanna studied Deborah closely. She had pretty dimples. Susanna touched her own cheeks and found her own dimples. She wondered if she'd ever meet this girl. As she handled each photograph, she felt as though Papà were offering her pieces of herself. From these fragments, she might make up a whole life.

"I've told them about you, Susanna."

"You have?" She held up the photographs. "All these people know about me?"

Papà nodded. "In my last letter home, I wrote about you."

"And what did they say?"

"I haven't gotten a letter back, but I know they'll be thrilled."

Susanna put her hand on his forearm.

She noticed Pina walking back and forth on the other side of the lemon tree, bouncing a Ping-Pong ball up and down on the paddle.

"Pina!" Susanna called to her. "Bring another chair. I have people to show you."

Pina carried the chair over, the legs scraping across the tiles.

Susanna handed her the photographs one by one:

"My grandmother . . ."

"My grandfather with Papà as a little boy . . ."

As Pina took the pictures, Susanna noticed her smile ever so slightly. "This girl looks like you," Pina said, holding up the photograph of Deborah.

"Yes," said Susanna, "I think she does."

The evening clouds blushed pink with sunset. Birds crossed the sky, calling to one another, returning home to their nests.

The Right Thing

ON RETURNING TO THE *ISTITUTO* after her solo trip out, Pina had found the front door unlocked. Clutching Mammina's note, she'd rushed down the hallway to the door of Suor Anna's office.

She hadn't knocked but had opened the door and marched in, announcing, "Here's something important." She dropped the note on Sorella's desk.

Sorella picked up the piece of paper. While Pina danced from one foot to the other—there'd been no bathrooms along the route—Sorella had read Mammina's words, then flipped to the other side to see the details of the bread receipt.

At the end, she'd smiled. "Your mother has done the right thing, Giuseppina. All these years, I've been waiting for her to come to this decision. On Sunday we'll have a large group of prospective parents."

"Oh!" Pina exclaimed. "Do you think someone will take me?"

"We can only hope," answered Suor Anna. "You are very pretty. But you must be on your best behavior."

And now, standing on the wooden steps in the *chiesa,* waiting to sing, Pina watched couples enter the church: the man with the black goatee and his slim wife in the polka-dot dress; the woman with the diamond-studded glasses and her husband, who stared at the ground, the man with . . .

"Look, Susanna," Pina said, "They've all come looking for me!"

"You'll have to choose between them when they fight over you," Susanna replied, elbowing Pina in the ribs.

Suor Vicenza raised her conductor's baton, and Pina, little shivers traveling up and down her spine, lifted her voice in song.

GLOSSARY

addio—good-bye

amo, amas, amat, amamus, amatis, amant (Latin)
I love, you (singular) love, he/she loves, we
love, you (plural) love, they love

armadietto—cupboard

aspirante—a woman who wants to become a nun,
the stage before becoming a postulant

Ave Maria—Hail Mary

baccalà—salty dried fish

bambina—baby girl

basso, bassi (plural)—street-level apartment

Befana—Christmas angel dressed as a witch

bellissima—beautiful

biscotti—Italian cookies

bosco—woods

buona sera—good evening

cannibale—cannibal

cannoli—tubes of pastry filled with sweet ricotta cheese

cappuccino—coffee with steamed milk

cara—dear

carabiniere—police officer

chiesa—church

diavolo, diavola (feminine)—devil

Dominus vobiscum./Et cum spirito tuo/Ite; Missa est/Deo gratias (Latin)—The Lord be with you/And with thy spirit/Go; the Mass is ended/Thanks be to God.

due—two

figlia—daughter

gelato—Italian ice cream

grazie—thank you

Il Vomero—a residential section of Naples

Istituto di Gesù Bambino—Institute of the Baby
  Jesus

lira, lire (plural)—unit of Italian money

luminari—luminaries, decorative lights

maestra—teacher (feminine)

Mammina—an endearment meaning Mommy

mari—seas

Maschio Angioino—a medieval castle in Naples

missal—a book containing all that is said and
  sung at Mass during the year

Mostra d'Oltremare—a large park on the outskirts
  of Naples

mulatta, mulatte (plural)—mulatto, person of
  mixed blood (feminine)

Nero, nera (feminine), *neri* (masculine plural)—
  black person, African American

nonna—grandmother

palazzo—palace, mansion

panini (plural)—rolls

papà—papa, dad

postulante—postulant, a woman in the second
stage of becoming a nun

prosciutto—a kind of Italian ham

risotto—a rice dish

scala quaranta—a card game

scusami—excuse me

sfogliatelle—Italian puff pastries

sirocco—a hot wind from Africa that blows
through southern Europe

Sorella, Sorelle (plural)—Sister

Spumoni—ice cream in layers, often with candied
fruit and nuts

stanza della compagnia—parlor

stigmata—marks or wounds resembling those of
Jesus on the cross

suora, suore (plural)—nun (shortened to *suor* when followed by name)

terrazzo—rooftop garden

tre—three

triste—sad

uno—one

zeppole di San Giuseppe—doughnut-like fried pastries made in honor of Saint Joseph's Day (March 19)

ACKNOWLEDGMENTS

I would like to acknowledge Daniella Cinque, whose childhood in a Naples convent inspired this story. I also acknowledge Goldfish Point Café in La Jolla where I wrote much of *Take Me with You*. Looking out at the ocean view from the little table in the back, I imagined the cliffs of Sorrento. Special readers were Sarah Wones Tomp and Gretchen Woelfle, who brainstormed endlessly and fruitfully. And finally, I acknowledge my editor and fellow writer, Deb Noyes Wayshak, for her encouragement, faith, and ability to deepen the story by asking just the right questions.